GUERILLA

The rubber and lumber tycoons were recruiting a private army of gunmen to chase the rebels out of southern Mexico. Lassiter went along for the action and the money, but he had another reason: the rebel leader was an old friend turned double-crosser. Hiding out in the jungles, backed by his guerillas, Betancourt thought he was safe —a thought that would be his last.

THE MAN FROM LORDSBURG

Lassiter rode up from Lordsburg to Abilene with money on his mind. Texas Jack Chandler—the richest, meanest bastard in the Lone Star State— was on the trail, heading north with a huge herd of cattle, and a fortune in gold. All that stood be- tween Lassiter and the biggest haul of all time was Chandler—and the most vicious rag-tag army of killers ever gathered together in one place.

JACK SLADE

GUERILLA
and
THE MAN FROM LORDSBURG

LEISURE BOOKS   NEW YORK CITY

A LEISURE BOOK

Published by

Dorchester Publishing Co., Inc.
6 East 39th Street
New York, NY 10016

Printed in the United States of America

THE
MAN FROM LORDSBURG

Chapter One

Lassiter was in Lordsburg when the telegraph came from Cassie McCord. After he read it, he rode to the nearest railroad at Curzon City and sold his horse. Shouldering his saddle and rifle, he bought a roundabout ticket to Abilene, Kansas.

It took him four days to get there, with changes at Volper Junction and Fort Marston. On the way, he played poker with a drummer, a retired cavalry captain with a bad cough, and a gun salesman. The gun salesman got off at a place called Mineville, and his place in the game was taken by a talky newspaper reporter who said he'd come West to look for local color.

The newspaper writer asked Lassiter if he'd care to have his life story, which he guessed was pretty colorful, put down on paper. Lassiter explained that he was a Mormon missionary and there wasn't much to tell. The consumptive captain smiled and the newspaper writer didn't ask any more questions.

It was dark when the train pulled into the Abilene depot, and Lassiter was good and sick of poker and stale cigar smoke when he stepped down and stretched his long legs.

Abilene sure as hell had changed. Fifteen years before he'd come through here with a posse of Kansas Jayhawkers riding hard behind him. That was when the town was just a wide place in the road. Now it was blazing with light and shaking with noise. Long before the train pulled into the depot, there was the deep lonesome sound of thousands of Texas longhorns bawling in the loading pens up ahead. The whole town smelled of cow.

He walked along Texas Street, the main stretch, looking for the Brazos Hotel. Abilene was in Kansas, but with hundreds of cowboys in town it was more like Fort Worth on a Saturday night. Out in front of the hotel a young Texas drover with a wispy yellow mustache and crossed gunbelts was calling a big cavalry sergeant a no-good Yankee bluebelly son of a bitch. Lassiter stepped around them and went inside.

The room clerk had a bald head and a waxed mustache. After putting fresh points on his fool mustache, he checked the register and agreed that a room had been reserved in advance by a Miss Smith. He smiled knowingly at Lassiter and Lassiter smiled back. After that the clerk didn't think the name or the situation was so funny. But he did say that Lassiter was lucky to get a room, any kind of room in Abilene. The clerk seemed quite proud of Abilene, and Lassiter knew the little bastard was fishing for a dollar. He didn't give it to him.

Upstairs, Lassiter locked the door and got a pint bottle of whiskey from his saddlebag and lay down on the bed. The pillow was thin and dirty, but it was better after he put his saddle behind it as a prop. After he built himself a smoke, he lay down again and drank some of the whiskey. While he drank he studied a weary-looking chromo hanging crooked on the wall. It was called Stag at Bay, and he had seen it in dirty and clean hotel rooms all the way from Butte, Montana to Benson, Arizona. In some hotels there was a choice—Stag at Bay or Custer's Last Stand. This was the first Stag he had seen with bullet holes in him.

Lassiter pulled at the bottle and waited for Cassie to show up. She hadn't said when that would be, and Lassiter wasn't anxious, about that or anything. Cassie had asked him to come, and here he was. She had mentioned big money, and that was enough to bring Lassiter all the way from Lordsburg or the hottest corner of hell. He didn't ask himself what Cassie might have in mind. Time enough to think about that when he knew what it was.

He drew his gun and got off the bed. There was another knock. By then Lassiter was out of the way of the door. "Miss Smith?" he called out. Cassie didn't have much imagination.

"You look older," Cassie said when she came

in. "Or maybe you look the same. I don't know which."

"No need to argue about it," Lassiter said. "You look fine, Cassie." That was lying a little, not much. Cassie looked all right, but not fine, not the way he remembered her from the old days. She'd be in her early thirties now, still beautiful but sort of tired, as if some of the wildness had been knocked out of her. Even so, there was still a lot of woman behind the tired blue-green eyes, underneath the black dress. The dress was quiet and it looked like it had cost a whole lot more than the glittery, beaded dresses he'd seen her in, back in El Paso when he'd killed Jimmy Voss to get her.

"Don't say it, Lassiter," Cassie said, opening the drawstring of a silk bag and taking out a square bottle and two glasses.

"I won't," Lassiter said. "Whatever it is."

She put down the glasses and poured two drinks. "This is brandy, all the way from Chicago. We never drank that in the old days."

"The old days weren't so bad," Lassiter said. "Was that what you didn't want me to say?"

Cassie poured another drink. "I guess they weren't so bad. They were all right when they happened. Now they stink."

"Not worse than Abilene," Lassiter said.

Cassie smiled, feeling better. "That isn't cowshit you smell, Lassiter. That's money."

"My favorite smell," Lassiter said, and they both laughed.

"We had one hell of a time, didn't we, Lassiter? It was like we could live forever. Taking

8

what we wanted. Moving on when we got tired of a town."

"I still do, little sister," Lassiter said.

Cassie said, "It's different for a woman. Anyway, it's different for me. Time for me to get away from the guns and the killing and the whiskey and the cowshit."

She looked at him. "Let me ask you something. Why in hell did you ride off like that?"

"Must of been something important," Lassiter said, reaching for her.

"You bastard!" she said, but didn't put up any more fight than that when he pulled her down on top of the sagging bed. "I came here to talk business."

"Then talk, honey."

"Later," Cassie said.

It was much later because doing what they had to do took some time, the way they were feeling, all those years to make up.

Glistening with sweat, Cassie sat up in bed and began to fix her hair. She reached down and touched Lassiter. "You may be older," she said, "but the years haven't softened you a bit."

Lassiter figured since he had his pants off he might as well stay in bed. Cassie got up and got dressed. With the pink in her cheeks she looked more like the old Cassie McCord who had every hard-case in El Paso scratching on her door. She still hadn't said anything about why he was here in Abilene. Right now, this was Cassie's show and he wasn't about to spoil it for her. She was what they called dramatic, like Lily Langtry, only more so.

Finally, she stopped walking up and down. "What does a cow cost in Texas?" she asked, smiling.

"Five or ten dollars, teacher, depending on the cow and the year and the time of year."

Cassie asked next, "And what does a good Texas cow fetch in Abilene?"

Lassiter was beginning to get it. "Twenty-five, thirty dollars, depending again," he said.

"Thirty," Cassie said decisively. "And when you multiply six thousand by thirty, what do you get?"

"A lot of money," Lassiter answered, knowing exactly how much.

Cassie had worked herself up to another drink. "I'm talking about a hundred and eighty thousand, maybe more. Does that sound big enough for you?"

Lassiter asked for the bottle back.

"That's the smallest it can be," Cassie said. "The least is what I said and the most could be two hundred thousand. What do you think of that?"

Lassiter sat up in bed. "I think it's just fine," he said. "Six thousand cows must be the biggest herd come up from Texas. I thought fifty-five hundred was the record fetched by King and Kenedy back in '76."

"This is the biggest," Cassie told him, sounding sure of herself. "The biggest and the most money Abilene is likely to see for some time. Texas Jack Chandler's boys are driving the herd in right now. Ought to be here in about a week. About three thousand cows belong to Jack, the rest to small ranchers who throw in with him. You know how Texas Jack works."

"I know he won't be easy to rob," Lassiter said. He decided he'd been wrong in thinking that Cassie had no imagination, because Texas Jack Chandler was about the most unrobbable man in the State of Texas, or any other state or territory. Dick King and Mifflin Kennedy were the biggest cattlemen in Texas, which made Chandler second biggest, but nobody would be likely to deny that Texas Jack was the biggest and meanest son of a bitch who ever came up the Chisholm Trail. On the surface he was as jovial as a tinhorn politician. Underneath he was as dangerous as a sick snake. He had put together his first herd of wild, unbranded cows in the brush country of South Texas. Now, fifteen years later, he was working on his second million, and was still a loudmouth, conniving, cow stealing bastard.

"What do you think?" Cassie asked.

"I'm thinking it'll take men and money to bust open Texas Jack's money-box," Lassiter said. "Now suppose you fill me in and we'll think about it some more."

Cassie explained that Texas Jack wasn't with the herd, which was moving up from the south. Chandler had arrived in town ahead of the drive. Then he had gone east to Kansas City in his new parlor car to bring back the chief buyer for one of the big meat packing plants, a man named Woodruff.

"Woodruff has the money," Cassie explained, "and Jack doesn't want anything to happen to

11

it. Besides, he wants to show off his private train, make a big hurraw for the money man. They're supposed to get back here about the time the herd does. Texas Jack swaps the cows for the money—then we take the money."

Lassiter liked her nerve. "It sounds downright easy the way you say it. But listen. If the money's on the train, why not take the train?"

"Not this train, Lassiter. "I know what I'm talking about. Texas Jack may be just a poor cow millionaire, but he's better guarded than President Hayes. The windows of the parlor car are made of Bismarck glass you can't shoot through, and the doors are heavy steel faced with oak. Three guards ride in the parlor car itself, some more in the caboose. The caboose has a Gatling gun mounted on a swivel."

"No wonder President Hayes is kicking himself," Lassiter said. "You're probably right about the train. Tell me this—where does he keep this train when he's in town?"

Cassie said, "He has it switched to a siding down by the loading pens. It stinks there, but Jack says he likes the smell of cowshit. Says it's really the smell of money."

"That's where you latched on to that expression," Lassiter remarked. "I wonder how he smells himself."

Cassie got mad. "What's that supposed to mean?"

Lassiter waved the half-empty bottle at her, making a peace sign. "Not a thing, sis. Just talk."

Cassie stopped fooling with her hair. She

sighed and sat down on the edge of the bed. "I guess you know anyway," she said. "Or you know something. Jack and me were together three years. This is the third year I been with him. Least it was. I guess I was all right when Jack was just a dirty trailherder up from Texas. Now he's got all kinds of big plans, sinking his money into businesses back East. And I'm just a wore out whore."

There was nothing to say and Lassiter didn't say it. Women were all the same—sore losers. Maybe that's why they were no good at cards or any other kind of game. They walked into the game with their eyes and their legs open, then when the game went sour, so did they. He didn't feel sorry for Cassie. For three years she'd been swinging on Texas Jack's middle leg, and now she was getting set to use the knife on him.

Cassie's blue-green eyes glittered. "You know what that son of a bitch did! He handed me five hundred dollars for three goddamned years. Now what in hell am I going to do with five hundred dollars?"

"You're going to give it to me," Lassiter said, "so we can get this new business of ours started."

Chapter Two

The mob in the telegraph office was keeping two telegraphers busy. It looked like everybody in Abilene was trying to send a message. They were all talking about Texas Jack's herd and making a lot of noise. After Lassiter finished writing the messages he wanted to send, he took the yellow sheets to the old man in charge and told him to get them off right away.

The old man was bald on top and fringed on the sides, like a monk. His green eyeshade kept slipping, and so did his temper.

"Rush! Rush! Everybody's in a rush these days," the old man whined. "And for what, mister? Let me ask you that."

He stopped complaining when Lassiter reached across the counter and stuffed a folded greenback in his vest pocket. The old man had false teeth carved out of bone, the kind nobody ever saw any more except in swaybacked station agents' mouths. The old buzzard smiled a dollar's worth.

"Speaking of the telegraph," he cackled, "you know what that writer fella, Truro, said back in Concord, Mass? That fella said it could be that Maine and Texas don't have nothing important to communicate. That's a good one, ain't it?"

"Right away means now," Lassiter warned him. "Now you do it, grampaw."

"Just hold your horses, young fella," the old man grumped, "and we'll see if you got this telegraph business straight. A lot of you fellas come in here and send telegraphs and then come back and say you didn't say what you said in the first place."

Lassiter waited while the old man read through the five names and addresses:

T. J. Murphy. Murphy's Saloon. Fort Smith. Arkansas.

Juno Flowers. Locksmith. Denver. Colorado.

Oren Kingsley. Bella Union Hotel. Omaha. Nebraska.

Calvin Moseley. Moseley Leather Company. Amarillo. Texas.

Howey Winters. c/o The Midway Theatre. St. Louis. Missouri.

The message was the same on all five telegrams: *Big business opportunity. Abilene. Kansas. Lassiter. Brazos Hotel.*

Lassiter told the old bastard that was fine. He told him he'd be back later for the replies, if any. Like he had told Cassie McCord the night before, time was getting short. If they were to

16

do the job right, they would need good men fast. If they were going to take that hundred and eighty-thousand from Texas Jack, they would need more than a bunch of fast guns. Fast guns were a nickel-for-six in Kansas. That was the trouble with fast guns—all gun and no head.

Picking his way across Texas Street through the churned-up mud and cowshit, he listened to the kids hawking copies of the *Abilene-Sentinel*. In Abilene, Texas Jack's herd was more important than the Second Coming of Christ. Scraping off his boots on the boardwalk, Lassiter thought: just what Abilene needs—six thousand more cows! But he wasn't about to complain. The way he and Cassie had figured it, they would take half of the hundred and eighty-thousand and let the others split up their ninety-thousand five ways. Lassiter's share would come to forty-five thousand, and for that kind of money they could fill the Missouri River with cowshit and he'd swim across it with a rose in his teeth.

He went into the first restaurant he saw and asked the waitress for ham and eggs, and she laughed at him. She looked like a Swede farmer from up Nebraska, and she spoke like it. "You must be new in town," she sassed him. It was the same with the flapjacks he ordered. The bulge-chested Swede said it was steak or nothing, but he had a choice. He could have steak with pinto beans or steak without. Lassiter wondered what she was like in bed, but he didn't ask her.

Some feeder had left a copy of the *Abilene-*

Sentinel on the table and he looked through it while his steak was burning. There was an engraving of Texas Jack Chandler on the front page. The millionaire cattleman looked less like a dressed-up bear than he normally did. The engraver had trimmed Jack's double-barreled mustache and taken two inches from his pugnacious jaw, adding them to his forehead. But it was Texas Jack, sure enough, the famous white Stetson stuck on the back of his head, and flashing the same bucktooth smile.

Among other remarkable things, the *Abilene-Sentinel* declared that Texas Jack Chandler would make a fine Vice President. Texas Jack, an outstanding example of the go-getter spirit, was quoted as saying that he had started in the cattle business with nothing but a horse, a saddle, and ten dollars cash money. Lassiter figured he had stolen the ten dollars.

He ate slowly, killing time. According to the *Sentinel,* which was publishing daily bulletins, Texas Jack's record-breaking herd was due to arrive in five or six days. Cassie had said a week. That gave him one less day than he thought he had. Time didn't mean much if he didn't start getting answers to those five telegram messages. All he had so far was the sketchiest kind of plan. The fact was, it wasn't even a plan, just a hard look at the situation. The way Lassiter saw it, it involved cows, horses, a train, a safe, and probably some killing. That was how it looked right now.

T. J. Murphy was one of the best horse-handlers in the Army before he went to Leavenworth for ten years for killing a man in a saloon. A vicious, moody drunk, Murphy loved horses and hated men; out of prison three years, he had worked with Lassiter on several big jobs. That was how he managed to buy the saloon in Fort Smith.

Juno Flowers knew locks and safes. A shaky, nervous man, the only time he seemed to steady up was when there was danger. He seemed to need it. Lassiter thought it had something to do with the war. Flowers operated a locksmith business in Denver between jobs.

Oren Kingsley was an old railroad man who had worked at everything from track layer and gandy dancer to locomotive engineer and section boss. If he hadn't wrecked a train and killed seventy-three people, he might have been president of the railroad by now. They said he had worked with the James boys, robbing trains after he got out of jail. Recently, he had been tending bar in the Bella Union Hotel in Omaha.

Old Calvin Moseley, now running a harness and leather shop in Amarillo, had worked as a trail boss for Washington Malone, and, later, Charles Goodnight. Once they hanged him for running off stock. He dangled ten minutes before a tame Indian happened along and cut him down. They hadn't bothered to hang him again. As Charles Goodnight always said, a man with a twisted neck was living proof that it didn't pay to rustle cows.

Thinking about it while the waitress brought the third cup of coffee, Lassiter decided he didn't like any of them; but the one he liked least was Howey Winters, or Handsome Howey, as they called him behind his narrow back. Lassiter knew Winters from all over. Handsome Howey was a trick shooter, a perfect, natural, nerveless shot with both hands, with rifle or pistol, and he was also a hired killer. When he wasn't killing somebody he didn't know, he dazzled the rubes at the Midway Theatre in St. Louis, in which he had a small interest.

A real nice bunch of fellas, Lassiter decided with a sour smile. Every one of them twisted or gone wrong in one way or another. Just the kind of men he needed to take away that bale of money from Texas Jack. Taking it wouldn't be easy, no matter how many or what kind of men he had. Fort Riley was only twenty miles away, and though robbing Texas Jack wasn't strictly an Army matter, the Army would probably get into it somehow because of Chandler's important connections.

It was still too early to go back to the telegraph office. It was nine o'clock in the morning and the saloons and whorehouses along the gaudy main stretch of Texas Street were running wide open. Lassiter paid for his breakfast and took a walk down by the marshal's office. Up ahead of him on the boardwalk two deputies were dragging a prisoner toward the jail. Most of the fingers on the prisoner's right hand had been chopped off neatly below the knuckle. The wounded man was still drunk and didn't know or didn't want to know that his fingers were missing. He kept clawing his empty holster and that made the bleeding worse.

Lassiter followed the trail of blood down to the marshal's office and jail, and stood looking at the old wanted posters out front. While he was doing it, the marshal, a barrel-chested man in his fifties, came out and looked at the blood on the boardwalk. He went back inside without taking any interest in Lassiter. Lassiter grinned at some of the familiar faces in the sheaf of yellowing posters, but there was no picture or description of him. This far north he didn't think there would be, unless there were newer ones inside. And there was no easy way to check that.

Besides the marshal, he figured, a town like Abilene would have five or six deputies, with maybe four extra men to handle the cuttings and shootings on Saturday night. That was the professional law, and by itself it wasn't so bad. But when you added in Texas Jack's hired gunmen and the soldiers at Fort Riley, and allowed for the fact that Jack Chandler was Abilene's leading citizen, the odds went way up. For a smaller take it wouldn't be smart to go up against all that gun power; but in this game, Lassiter figured, the money pretty well balanced the odds.

The thought occurred to Lassiter that he might not be the only interested party in town. The smell of money brought them in from all directions, just as it had brought him, and that was something else he had to consider. Competition from another gang could interfere with his operation even more quickly than the law. He didn't know many gangs with brains or guts enough for a job like this, but you never knew. It was something to think about.

He walked down to the depot, then past that to the huge loading pens where the longhorns were prodded aboard cattle cars for a one-way jaunt to the slaughterhouse. Extra trains had been brought in to clear the pens of cattle. New pens were being built, and there were freshly printed posters with the ink still wet stuck up everywhere. The posters said: *WELCOME TEXAS JACK*. Lassiter figured there hadn't been so much excitement since Sherman burned Atlanta.

The office of the Texas Jack Chandler Cattle Company was in a two-story frame building. Just beyond it was a short railroad siding with a wide gate. That was the place Cassie had mentioned. And that was where the money would be. The siding was empty now.

Making a map in his head, Lassiter walked through the pens, then made a wide swing and came back into town by one of the side streets. He drifted down Texas Street on the west side of the street, past the Drover's Hotel, past filled-up saloons with names like Old Fruit and The Pearl. Cassie had a room at the Thompson Hotel, the best place in town. Down past that was the Alamo Saloon where Wild Bill and John Wesley Hardin had their famous showdown. Lassiter went into the Alamo, figuring to kill another hour before he went back to the telegraph office.

The Alamo was something to see. They called it the Alamo to bring in the Texas Trade, and it looked like the name was a success. The bar was as long as a Mexican funeral, and ten times as lively. Five bartenders, working with both hands, just about kept even with the demand for drinks. On a raised platform the loudest band Lassiter ever heard was topping off the uproar with piano, fiddle, trumpet, and bull fiddle. All the tunes in the Alamo were "Texas" tunes. The band buffaloed its way through "Lorena" and gathered speed with "Lone Star Girl."

Lassiter elbowed his way to the bar and ordered a beer. A man he didn't know turned to him and said, "Well now, ain't that Texas Jack something? Ain't that old boy something." Lassiter said he sure as hell was. The man turned away, still running off at the mouth. There was nobody Lassiter knew to talk to. The competition, if there was any, was keeping out of sight.

Three beers and four smokes later, at eleven o'clock, Lassiter left the Alamo and went back to the telegraph office. When he gave his name, the old man cackled and said, "You got right lively business associates, mister. The last one just sent a reply five minutes ago."

Chapter Three

Lassiter didn't do anything special while he waited for the others to get there. He lay on his bed and smoked, nipped on a bottle, and cleaned his guns. When he got sick of that he slept. The surest way to get noticed in any town was to stay holed up in his room all the time, so when he had enough of the hotel he went down to one of the saloons and sat in on a poker game. He won some, then lost some of it back.

The big-tit Swede waitress had taken a fancy to him, and he was all for that. Without being asked, she told him her name was Marta Lindstrom. She liked him so much he could have ham and eggs, if he came to the restaurant early or late enough. Miss Lindstrom explained in her back country Minnesota accent that the other customers would get mad if they saw him wolfing down ham and eggs while they had to make do with the same old standby—fresh, tough steak and pinto beans.

Lassiter couldn't recall any reason why he should dislike Swedes—he had killed a man once named Charlie Clingman, but maybe he was a German, not a Swede—and he was ready to do anything to get away from that goddamned steak. Besides, this Swede girl with the hourglass figure wasn't as bad as having a redhot Comanche arrowhead shoved up his ass. Butter and eggs had made her hefty, but she was a damn sight better than the pock-faced saloon girls along Texas Street.

Marta's widowed mother owned the restaurant and they lived upstairs. While the mother snored in the next room, Lassiter ate the ham and eggs the top-heavy Swede girl fixed for him, and later he straddled her on a curve-backed sofa that threatened to collapse under their weight. Lassiter decided he liked that as much or even more than the ham and eggs.

They got up and Marta apologized for having only whisky to offer him, not aquavit like her dead father had made on their fine farm up in Minnesota. Lassiter didn't know what in hell she was talking about. He said the whisky was fine.

The Swede girl was dreamy and Lassiter drank fast. It was good to have a lot of whisky when you finished with a woman and had to listen to her talk, because you figured it might be handy to have her around again. The old woman in the next room stopped snoring and started to cough. Lassiter hoped the old biddy would stay asleep. Sheriffs, back-shooters, bounty hunters,

Comanches, and whores with knives he was ready to face. White-haired Swede widows and mothers were something else.

Marta Lindstrom filled Lassiter's glass again and asked him if he had enough to eat. Lassiter said he was as tight-bellied as a poisoned pup, but if she let him wait a while he might like to have a second helping of something else. He meant it as a compliment and the girl took it that way, after about an hour had passed.

Lying there, Lassiter thought he might go down to the Alamo and drink some whisky and play a little poker before he turned in. Twice in two hours wasn't much with some women. With this iron-thighed Swede it was enough or nearly enough.

Marta sighed, got up, and put on her dress. "Why is it," she asked no one in particular, "that the men who have the money don't have the other thing?"

Thinking of his forty-five thousand to be, Lassiter said, "That ain't altogether right, sis."

"Well, you ain't rich, are you?"

"Not in the fleshy commodities of this world, honey."

"Like hell you aren't," the Swede girl said. "But what I want is the firm flesh and the big money. That's what I want and that's what I aim to get."

Lassiter said there was no reason why they shouldn't get together while she was waiting, and the Swede girl agreed.

The way Swede girls and certain mothers are, she asked him again if he had enough to eat.

Lassiter said he had enough ham and eggs, if that was what she meant. The girl blushed, and Lassiter buttoned up his pants and went down to his poker game.

It wasn't much of a game and Lassiter drank no more than a quarter of a pint of whisky before he pulled off his boots and went to bed.

Murphy got to Abilene before the others. Drifting through the depot, Lassiter saw the big Irishman get off the train. A colored bag-carrier ran forward to snag the Irishman's single bag. Murphy looked mean-tempered and sick with last night's whisky. He hit the colored man with the side of the bag and sent him flying. "Leave off, Rastus," Lassiter heard the big horse-handler say. The Negro scurried out of Murphy's way, eyeballs rolling.

The best Lassiter could do was to get two rooms for the five of them. It had taken an extra twenty dollars to get that much. Personally, Lassiter wouldn't like to bunk in with any of them, especially Murphy and Winters. He followed the Irishman along Texas Street. Murphy was the biggest man in sight, getting a bit old now but still tough as chuckwagon steak, and he walked as if he knew it. All those years in the cavalry must have given the Irishman a hate for wide-brimmed hats. Lassiter had never seen him wearing anything but a curve-sided derby.

Lassiter walked on past the hotel to the Alamo Saloon. He stayed there most of the morning, drinking and playing poker. Later in the day he got his horse and rode out along the railroad right of way, in the direction of Junction City and Fort Riley. Texas Jack's train would be coming back that way. It was getting dark when he rode back into Abilene.

The next day Winters, Kingsley, and Flowers arrived. The day clerk, with the waxed mustache and itchy palms, told him when he came down for breakfast. Lassiter told him he was doing a fine job of room clerking, to keep up the good work.

Lassiter wanted to think, and he couldn't do that with the Swede girl fussing over him. So he drank bad coffee in a three-stool hole-in-the-wall run by a one-legged veteran. After that he had the kid at the livery stable saddle his horse.

This time he rode with the rails going south. A general plan was coming together in his head. That was how he usually worked. The thing to do was look the situation over real good; when it came time for doing instead of talking, a plan would more or less suggest itself. Lassiter usually liked to work in country less thickly settled than central Kansas. Sometimes a mob of farmers with shotguns and pitchforks could be as much trouble as the best organized posse.

When he got back it was late, and the night clerk told him that Calvin Moseley had just come in on the last train. Lassiter hunted up the kid who swept up around the hotel and sent a message over to Cassie at the Thompson Hotel. Then he went upstairs.

Handsome Howey Winters opened the door and Lassiter saw they were all there. Already the room was thick with tobacco smoke and whisky stink. Most of the whisky stink was coming from Murphy, who looked red-eyed and truculent as ever.

"How do, Howey?" Lassiter asked Winters, coming in. "How's the murder business these days?"

Winters had been raised in a rotting wooden tenement on the St. Louis docks, and he looked like what he was—a vicious, pasty-faced city rat. Handsome Howey's taste in clothes ran to brownish suits with yellow checks and Jefferson ankle-shoes. Like the Irishman, Winters always wore a derby hat.

"A bit slow lately," Winters said. He sneered at Lassiter's trail-worn duds. "But I'm still a ways from being a hobo."

"I'm real delighted to hear that," Lassiter told him. He didn't offer to shake hands with any of them. Old Cal Moseley, who liked to play the old Texas cowhand when he wasn't off stealing cows or back-shooting some rider, stuck out his leathery hand. Lassiter ignored it.

Juno Flowers, the safe blower, looked as morose and shaky as ever. He looked at Lassiter and didn't say anything. One good thing about Juno—he was quiet. And that was all you could say for him.

Murphy was hogging one bottle all to himself. There was another bottle and some glasses on the dresser. Oren Kingsley had been fixing himself a drink when Lassiter came in. He filled the glass all the way up and put it away in one gulp. Going down, it made him shudder. Lassiter wondered how much liquor Kingsley had taken aboard the night he killed those seventy-three people in the train wreck.

"Good to see you, Lassiter," Kingsley said.

Lassiter nodded.

The old cane rocker creaked under Murphy's huge bulk. The Irishman drank straight from the bottle. Murphy was the kind of big-mouth clodhopper who would knock the neck off a bottle even when it was just as easy to pull out the cork.

"Jesus, boys," he said. "If it isn't Colonel Lassiter finally come to pay us a call. Such an honor. Think of it, boys."

To Lassiter he said, "What in hell's the matter with you, cowboy? I been sitting 'round here most of two bloody days. Couldn't you least have the manners to come up and have a drink with a man, and say hello?"

"If you were lonely, T. J.," Lassiter said, "why didn't you go out and stomp somebody to death?"

The Irishman heaved himself out of the chair. Even by himself he would have made the hotel room look small. "You got a bad mouth, Lassiter," he said. "A dirty mean mouth and it gets bad instead of better. Maybe I'm the boy to give it a whole new shape."

Lassiter walked over to the dresser and poured himself a drink. His back was to the Irishman. "Sit down, Timothy J.," he said easily. "I don't like you and you don't like me, but that ain't why we're here. Later you're welcome to fix my bad mouth if you have a mind to."

31

The chair creaked as the Irishman sat down. Lassiter turned around. "Here's looking at you," he said.

"May it choke you," Murphy said.

"Why are we here?" Howey Winters asked. Winters had pale hair and eyes. Everything about him was pale, cold as a gravestone by moonlight. His hands were long and pale and once in a while they twitched as if closing over the butts of guns you couldn't see.

Lassiter drank some of the whisky paid for with Cassie's money. Murphy was red and Winters was slug-belly white. Old Cal Moseley was a sneaking thief and hypocrite. Kingsley had killed seventy-three men, women and children, and he still whined about the bad luck life had brought him. Juno Flowers was a shifty-faced weasel. They were a fine bunch of men. Just down home folks.

"What about it, Lassiter?" Winters asked again. "You mentioned this here business opportunity."

"It's big," Lassiter said, stalling to give Cassie time to get there. He mentioned Texas Jack and the $180,000.

"Holy Jesus," Murphy said, shaking his head.

Lassiter looked at Winters.

Cal Moseley massaged his twisted neck and said, "Well, I'll be a son of a bitch."

"This one could get us killed," Howey Winters said.

There was no comment from Juno Flowers and Oren Kingsley.

Lassiter explained about Cassie McCord.

There was no use trying to go ahead unless he did.

There was a knock on the door. Winters took a long-barreled .32 from under his coat so fast that Lassiter hardly saw his hand move.

"Open it," Lassiter said.

Kingsley opened the door and Cassie came in.

"A woman!" Winters protested. "A god-damned woman!" He turned to Lassiter, putting the gun away. "Oh no, Lassiter, I don't want any part of this."

"Who is this fool?" Cassie asked, not a bit put off.

"You want a drink, Cassie?" Lassiter asked.

"Not that slop. I brought my own. Even brought a clean glass."

"Be Jesus, this is a new one on me," T. J. Murphy said, grinning like the raunchy old bastard he was.

Cal Moseley tried to offer the lady his chair. Lassiter told him to stay where he was.

"Thanks anyway," Cassie said.

Old Cal bobbed his twisted neck like a turkey trying to dodge the Thanksgiving axe.

"Shit, Lassiter," Winters said, glaring at Cassie. "You ain't going to tell me this deal is run by a woman."

Lassiter took his time about fixing himself another drink. After he poured the drink he built a smoke, and he took longer doing that.

"Howey," he said finally, striking a woodie on the top of the dresser. "I guess I'll just have to tell you again, since you wasn't listening when I told you on that first job we worked on together.

33

Any job I work on I run. I do the thinking. I do the talking. No woman—nobody—runs the show but me. You get that, do you, Howey?"

"I'm no fool," Winters snarled.

Murphy mimicked him. "I'm no fool. It's just that I'm the kind of a fella doesn't like girls. Now boys with soft asses is something else."

Winters' pale eyes narrowed. "You clodhopper son of a bitch," he said.

Murphy was drunk and he wasn't afraid of Winters. Drunk or sober, he wasn't afraid of anything. That was one of the things wrong with him, Lassiter decided. "Look, Howey," he said. "You don't like this deal—walk away from it. No hard feelings and there's the door."

Winters was still staring at Murphy, but he spoke to Lassiter. "I come a long way, friend. I'd like to listen."

Lassiter was getting sick of the cross talk. "You listen you know, Howey. Get in or get out. Take a minute to think about it. Only listen to this, sharpshooter, once you say in the only way out is dead."

Winters was scared of women and not much else. He wanted to kill the mouthy Irishman, but now he was talking to Lassiter. "I can break six marbles out of six," he said.

"Marbles don't shoot back," Lassiter informed him. "Now suppose we put the smart talk away and talk about this plan I have in mind."

Chapter Four

The big herd was still two days south of Abilene when Texas Jack's private train arrived from Kansas City. It didn't come in quietly, early in the morning or after dark, but on the stroke of noon. Lassiter figured that was about when it would be, but the town didn't know because Texas Jack hadn't set any special time. Jack was learning political tricks all right. Men without a dollar in their levis were all anxious and worked up about Jack Chandler's money.

Earlier that morning a wild rumor had gone around that the train had been run off the rails by a gang of bushwhackers led by Colonel Quantrill's crazy son. Quantrill had no son, at least none given to robbing trains, but the name still meant excitement in Kansas, and it gave the town something to talk about.

Going down to the Alamo, Lassiter saw a

troop of cavalry with a colonel up front heading for the railroad depot. The colonel had burnside whiskers and looked to be on an important errand. The troopers rode straight-backed in their saddles. Somehow they didn't seem to be as impressed with the occasion as the colonel. The colonel would be the Army's official greeter.

Lassiter plaped cards till eleven thirty, then finished his drink and sauntered down to the depot. Already, there was a mob of people there, mostly cowboys, and they were getting up a good head of steam on the bottles being passed around. Up on a wide platform draped with *WELCOME TEXAS JACK* banners, a brass band in gaudy uniforms were sweating in the sun. They had been there since eight o'clock that morning.

Lassiter played cards till eleven thirty, then and rolled a cigarette. Putting a match to it, he spotted Kingsley and Murphy drifting through the crowd. It wasn't hard to spot Murphy. The band had been drinking and the bandmaster looked ready to draw a gun on them when they bollixed up a fast run-through of "Zack, The Mormon Engineer." After he yelled at them for a while, with the mob of cowbops offering some salty comments of their own, the band did better with "The Old Chisholm Trail."

They were doing fine with "Dixie," the evergreen favorite of the trail hands, when a young rider came tearing down Texas Street yelling his head off. "Son of a bitch they're coming!" Some of the ladies sweating delicately under their parasols looked shocked. Way out on the prairie a hooter started blasting. The crowd yelled, then simmered down, and in the quiet that followed they could hear a locomotive bell clanging. Well, so much for Colonel Quantrill's crazy son, Lassiter thought.

The mayor of Abilene, followed by the sheriff and other town officials, bustled down to the depot. The colonel Lassiter saw earlier had dusted off his uniform and combed out his whiskers. When he climbed up on to the welcome platform and shook hands with the mayor, the band exploded with brassy sounds.

"Not yet, you bastards," the bandmaster roared, shaking with rage and excitement. The mayor's wife frowned at him. The music trailed off and the train bell got louder. The sound of money, Lassiter decided. He spotted Oren Kingsley again but Murphy wasn't to be seen. There was no sign of any competition in the crowd.

The train clanged to a stop and a blast of escaping steam drove the crowd back. "Now," the bandmaster roared. "Dixie" added to the uproar as Texas Jack Chandler, magnificent as Buffalo Bill Cody in gray broadcloth and white boots, swung down from the train. Texas Jack took his time getting down. He held onto the grip-handle with one hand and waved his famous white Stetson with the other.

Lassiter thought it would have been smarter of Texas Jack to have allowed his bodyguard, Dixon Quirly, to get down first. But Jack wasn't about to let anybody spoil his moment of glory, even if it meant taking a bullet from some crackpot with a real or imagined grudge. Lassiter knew what Texas Jack looked like. Right now he was more interested in Quirly. He didn't know Quirly: he knew about him. What he'd heard was good or bad, depending on whether you were behind Quirly's gun or in front of it.

Quirly was nothing like the man he killed for. Once upon a time he had been town marshal of Fort Griffin, and he still looked the way most town tamers did—quiet, soberly dressed in a black frock coat and string tie, slow moving. The light-blue eyes that looked out at the crowd were dead and expressionless. Even his gun rig was plain, like the man himself, just a single-action, rubber-handled Colt .45 in a worn holster.

Even if Lassiter didn't know about the score of men Dixon Quirly had killed, some legal, most not, he would have figured him as fast and deadly. Lassiter had a strong hunch that he'd have to kill Dixon Quirly before this business in Abilene was finished. And it wouldn't be all that easy.

Now Texas Jack had his arm around the big cattle buyer, Mathew Woodruff. Woodruff, a fat man with a high hat, looked put-off by all the attention. But Texas Jack gripped him around the shoulders and wouldn't let go. "Here's the man with the money," Jack kept yelling. "Now come on, folks, let's all say a big hello to your friend and mine—Mathew Woodruff."

The crowd did what it was told and, flanked by four of Quirly's gunmen and four town deputies, Texas Jack pulled the pink-faced moneybags toward the welcome platform.

The mayor was trying to make himself heard.

The bandmaster raised his hand to wipe the sweat off his face. The music began again, two different tunes at one time. The bandmaster snatched off his kepi and threw it at the man playing the tuba. The noise kept building up until Texas Jack, showing all his buck teeth in a huge grin, pulled his matched, pearl-handled forty-fives and fired into the air.

"Shut up, you mully-grubbers," he roared, "goddamn it to hell's fire—I told you shut up."

Jack grinned wider than ever to show he wasn't mad. The crowd loved it. Texas Jack whacked the mayor between the shoulder blades, knocking the wind out of him. "Now you just air out your paunch, your honor," he howled. "Spit it out, your excellency, only don't take too long about it. We got some serious drinking to do."

"Hurrah for Texas Jack," an old man yelled. The cheering started again. It stopped when Texas Jack held up his hand. He looked down at the old man who was dressed in a greasy canvas coat and sweat-crusted wool hat. The old man was so drunk he could hardly stand.

"How's every old thing, Stinky?" Chandler asked the rumpot. "Been into the sasparilla again, have you?"

The crowd thought that was the funniest thing since Clay Allison fell off that buckboard and broke his neck. The mayor made another crack at giving a speech.

Looking at the train, Lassiter saw that the side of the caboose had been cut away. The long slit was covered with a hinged steel plate that could be raised or lowered from inside. It was raised part way now, and Lassiter thought he could see the muzzle of the Gatling gun. Cassie had said the Gatling was mounted on a swivel. That would mean there was another firing slit on the other side of the caboose. Unless he was mistaken the walls of the caboose were plated inside with steel.

The mayor smiled weakly and mopped his forehead when Texas Jack stood up and told him to dry up. Chandler was a little more respectful with the colonel from Fort Riley, but he hurried him along too. "That's just dandy, Colonel," he allowed, winking at the crowd from behind the officer's back. "And we surely do appreciate every word you just said. If I had the doing of it I'd make you a general right here and now."

Lassiter watched Oren Kingsley moping along by the train, just a harmless old galoot interested in locomotives and such. Kingsley might not know much about anything else, but he knew about trains. A little later, while Texas Jack was funning with the crowd, he caught sight of Howey Winters far back in the crowd. The little killer was staring at Dixon Quirly, standing behind the chairs on the platform where the dignitaries sat.

Texas Jack was saying, "You folks didn't come here to listen to a lot of hot air. You come here today to have a good time. And, by the Texas Christ, that's what you going to have. I'm feeling right good today, ladies and you so-called gentlemen, and I want you to feel just as good.

To be serious for a single minute, and I promise it ain't going to be longer than that or shoot me, let me say when old Texas Jack Chandler makes money, the whole town of Abilene makes money. 'Cause if you think this herd of mine is something, you're wrong. Why it ain't but the beginning. Next time we going to cover the whole State of Kansas with cowshit . . ."

Texas Jack paused to catch his breath and the old man called Stinky yelled, "The minute's up, Jack. We going to have to shoot you."

The crowd roared at the old man, but Chandler held up his hand. "Harm not a hair on that greasy head," he hollered. "It so happens that Stinky's right."

Lassiter was getting sick of Texas Jack and his goddamned folksiness. If he'd known it was going to take this long, he'd have brought along a bottle. The thought of all that money eased his bad humor a bit.

Texas Jack had hauled Stinky up on the platform and the mayor and the colonel were trying to make the best of it. It sure as hell looked as if Texas Jack was building himself up to run for some public office. Lassiter watched Oren Kingsley move away from the train and out through the crowd.

The old man, Stinky, would have fallen off the platform if Texas Jack hadn't held him up. Texas Jack was a son of a bitch, but he knew how to please a crowd. "Now looky here, Stink," Texas Jack was saying. He snapped his fingers in front of the rumpot's glassy eyes. Stinky came to life for a moment and yelled, "Remember the Alamo!"

The crowd howled, no one there louder than Texas Jack. "Would that be the battle or the saloon?" he asked the old man.

"Bring on the booze," Stinky shouted just before his eyes closed all the way. Texas Jack threw him off the platform into the crowd, and they loved that too.

"You heard the man," Chandler called out. "Now everybody get themselves down to the Alamo and drink till you sick." Texas Jack paused and closed one eye. "Drinks are on me!"

Lassiter let the crowd rush by him before he started back for the hotel. When the mob thinned out, he saw the five buffalo hunters. Moving fast, he put a hay wagon between himself and the five men. Well, he thought, it had to happen.

He watched Morgan Harpe and his four brothers looking at Texas Jack's train. It had been a good three years since he'd run across the Harpe brothers down in Indian Territory. There had been six brothers then. Lassiter had killed Noah Harpe when all six of them had crept up on his camp at night and tried to do him in. The Harpes were like that. From the first day they'd climbed down out of the Ozarks they'd been murdering and stealing, but mostly murdering. It was said they would murder a man for an old pair of boots. Lassiter knew better than that. The Harpes would torture and murder a man for the fun of it.

Lassiter edged away from the wagon and

headed for the hotel without looking back. He knew damn well the Harpes hadn't come to Abilene to listen to Texas Jack sound off about how big he was. The Harpes weren't real buffalo hunters. It was more their style to wait till some other men loaded up their hides, then cut down on them. On the face of it, they were more suited to bushwhacking and night-crawling then robbing trains. They were just mean enough and dumb enough to try it, and spoil everything.

Moseley and Kingsley were upstairs. Kingsley wanted to talk about the train. Lassiter cut him off. "Not now, Oren," he said. "You go out and find Murphy and Winters. Never mind about Flowers. Tell them to get up here on the double."

Kingsley left without asking questions.

"Trouble?" Moseley asked.

"You know what Morgan Harpe and his brothers look like?" Lassiter demanded.

Cal Moseley whistled. "Yeah, I know how they look. I guess you do too, from what I hear."

"That ain't why I'm asking. They're down at the depot right now. I think the crazy bastards mean to rob that train. What I want you to do is keep an eye on them. If they ride out of town you follow. If they're still in the buffalo business, it's likely they have some wagons out on the prairie."

"What you aim to do, Lassiter?"

"What do you think?" Lassiter asked.

"That's what I thought," Cal Moseley said, fingering his scarred, twisted neck, as if the talk of trouble brought back bad memories.

"Don't waste time, Cal," Lassiter said. "We do this right or you can forget about the money. We move when you bring the good word."

Chapter Five

Howey Winters had a heavy Remington-Schuetzen rifle with a detachable stock. The little killer took the blanket-wrapped weapon out of his trunk, clicked the stock into place, and worked the under lever five times—fast.

The modified Remington-Hepburn was a beautiful gun. Lassiter had seen less than a dozen on the whole frontier. They used the Remington-Schuetzen in competition matches back east. It was a distance weapon, maybe the most accurate long gun in existence. Winters loved that gun as another man might love a woman. Lassiter didn't see any reason why he shouldn't. It had brought him a lot of murder money in his time.

With the big rifle in his hands, the pasty-faced killer was cockier than ever. "Look," he said to Lassiter, "what's all this fuss about these

Harpes. Man, the minute old Cal says where they're at, why I'll just lay out there under a blanket and douse their lights one by one. Five shots, five dead brothers. With my baby here I don't even have to get close. Those dirty birds won't know what hit them."

Lassiter didn't doubt for a moment that Handsome Howey could do it. Winters had knocked down more than a few good and bad men with the big rifle. He knew for a fact that Winters had dropped the Governor of a Mexican State and three of his aides at a range of nearly two hundred yards. Killing the Harpes would be no problem for Handsome Howey. Even if he missed one or two of them, which was god-damned unlikely, the rat-mouth killer would wait and nail them the first time they showed themselves.

"Winters is right," T. J. Murphy said, filling his glass so full it slopped over. "The little bas-tard is right, much as I hate to say it."

Winters knew better than to point the empty rifle at the Irishman. Instead he shook it, and said, "Look, you thick Mick . . ."

Murphy swallowed his drink and started to laugh. "Listen to the nance, will you."

"Everybody button up," Lassiter said, know-ing that Winters was right and piss-burned at himself for going against it. He was ready to do it, and do it ten times over, if there was absolu-tely no other way. He knew damn well there wasn't but the final say on that was up to the Harpes. Killing—five clean bullets from the big rifle—was too good for the Harpes. A man didn't have to be a killer like Winters or a savage like Murphy to know that. Even so, he didn't work that way.

The only one who didn't have an opinion was Juno Flowers. The morose safe-blower sat nursing his drink, following the talk with his unblinking eyes. Lassiter wished the others would use him as a model.

Kingsley said, "Trains, not guns, are my line. I'm no killer . . ."

"Only seventy-three people," Winters sneered.

"Are you crazy, man?" the Irishman asked. "Them Harpes'll cut you down soon as you show your face. After what you done to their brother, you'll be lucky if they kill you quick. Besides, and I speak as the greedy fella I am, you're putting this whole job in danger. Think of the money, Lassiter."

Winters had the same thought. "I didn't come all the way from St. Louis so's you can play gunfighter. Use your head, for Christ's sake."

Lassiter finished his drink. "I just listened to more talk than I usually have a mind to. You all had your say and now I'm going to tell you something straight off. You do what I say or get out. I don't give a stale dog turd if you came around the Horn for this job. Most likely you got the Harpes pegged right. Most likely and then some. And I don't give an ounce of shit for that. We do it my way or we forget the whole thing. That way is out."

Nobody moved and nobody said anything.

"All right then," Lassiter said.

There was a knock and Kingsley let Cal Moseley in. The old twist-neck stock thief had been riding hard. "Give him a drink," Lassiter ordered.

"They got a camp about three miles out," Mosely said. "Two wagons with mules. And five horses. That country is mighty flat out there. It ain't going be easy to ambush them fellas."

"What else?" Lassiter asked.

Moseley was indignant. "What else? What else is there?"

Juno Flowers didn't come along. Murphy, Winters, Kingsley, and Moseley left their horses in a narrow draw about a quarter of a mile from where the Harpe brothers were camped beside a creek. Kingsley stayed with the animals while the three others started out, crouched low at first, then, when it got too close for that, crawling on their bellies.

Lassiter gave them thirty minutes to get set. From the mouth of the draw where he sat astride his horse, he could see the Harpe camp plain enough. He was still piss-burned at himself for doing what he had to do. He didn't think at all about not doing it.

The Irishman took the left spot, Moseley the right, with Winters in the middle. When they were in position, Lassiter walked his horse out of the draw and headed toward the buffalo camp four hundred yards away. Before he had gone a quarter of that distance, somebody in the camp let out a yell. He began to wonder if he'd make it all the way to the wagons. Before he got close enough for them to see who he was, the Harpes might start shooting, figuring some kind of local law was coming out to take a look-see. There was a saying that a man didn't have to be shot more than once with a .54-caliber buffalo rifle. That big bullet powered by 90 grains of powder didn't just kill a man. It took him apart.

Lassiter kept closing the distance between himself and the camp. If he'd been more than one man, the Harpes would be hunkered down behind those wagons by now. One man didn't look like much, so they stepped out, bold and big.

Morgan Harpe was the oldest and biggest of the five brothers. With a beard that reached to his chest and hair that hung to his shoulders, the leader of the bushwhacking family might have been an Old Testament prophet, except nobody in the Bible or anywhere else stank like that. The wind was coming from the direction of the camp. It brought with it the stench of rotting buffalo hides and black blood.

Suddenly, Morgan Harpe yelled something Lassiter couldn't make out. He didn't have to understand the words. He knew what it was. The Harpes knew who was coming to call. Lassiter remembered what the Irishman said back in the hotel room: *You'll be lucky if they kill you quick.*

After the first outburst of yelling it was quiet. Lassiter kept coming. Now he knew how Custer must have felt when he woke up that morning and saw those five thousand Indians looking down his throat. They stood there in front of the wagons by the creek, waiting. Every man jack of them had a Big Fifty Sharps in his hands. It was hard to decide which of them looked dirtier and meaner. Morgan was supposed to be the smartest, but that wasn't saying much.

Morgan Harpe decided Lassiter was close enough. "Climb down and turn loose of that animal," the bushwhacker said, mild enough for someone looking at the man who'd killed his brother.

"You sure it's him?" one of the others asked.

"It's him certain," Morgan Harpe said. Lassiter decided the only thing worse than being killed by the Harpes would be having to live with them.

"Unbuckle the gunbelt," Morgan said, showing rotten, snaggled teeth in a wide smile. "Then we have ourself a nice visit. Just walked right in, didn't you. Look to be as how the Lord is answered our prayers. I told you to drop it, mister."

"No," Lassiter said. "No gun. I come here to talk. You want to listen or not."

Morgan Harpe still couldn't altogether believe it, having Lassiter fall at his feet this way. "Tell you the truth, mister," he drawled in his Ozark way. "I been looking for you so long I don't rightly know what I wants to do first. Only believe this good—you going to suffer for what you done to little Noah."

Lassiter recalled that "little" Noah stood six-one and weighed two hundred pounds. And, excepting the rest of the Harpes, a meaner man never burned a homestead. Lassiter said, "I

50

guess little Noah got what was coming to him. Night-crawling a man's camp that way. I just wish it could have been more of you, Morgan."

Lassiter didn't know the names of the other Harpes. One of them, maybe the youngest, raised his rifle. "I claim his boots," he announced.

"Ease up there, brother," Morgan said. "After the way he done Noah—you want to just shoot him. The Comanches wouldn't do some of the things I have in mind for this fella. Only that can wait a bit."

Morgan Harpe asked, "What was that you wanted to talk about. Speak your piece before we take off your pants."

Lassiter said it all together. "You're here to have a go at Jack Chandler's pay-off money. So am I. I think I can do it and you can't. Killing homesteaders and selling Indians to the Mexicans as slaves is one thing. You boys are good at that. Why don't you stick to it?"

Morgan Harpe said with a broad grin, "You mean you ain't even ready to split half the money whould we decide to leave this lay, which, naturally, we ain't about to do. Well, listen here, friend, you couldn't buy back your life with twice the money Jack's got. Oh no, sir, you ain't going to die this day, could be not even tomorrow. But we going to start soon with the cutting and burning and you going to eat your knackers and say you like it. Now does that answer your question?"

"Sure," Lassiter said, and shot Morgan Harpe twice through the chest. Out behind him two

Winchesters started to crack and there was the boom-boom-boom of Howey Winters' big rifle. Morgan was dead when he hit the ground and the four other brothers dropped like stones. Two of them weren't altogether dead. Lassiter swung his gun and put bullets through their heads. Just to make sure, he reloaded and did the same for the rest of them.

Howey Winters came through the tall grass at a run. The little killer's eyes were bright with excitement. He slapped the curved stock of the Remington-Schuetzen, saying, "How'd you like that? What d'you think of that? You see the way I dropped the sons of bitches?"

Lassiter looked at him coldly and Winters shut up. "Turn loose the animals," he told Cal Moseley when he and Murphy got there.

"Had fun, did you Howey?" the Irishman jeered. "Just as good as straddling a woman, ain't it?"

"Drop it, T. J.," Lassiter warned him.

Kingsley brought up the horses and they headed back toward Abilene. The bit of business with the Harpes couldn't have gone smoother. Time had been wasted, but there was no helping that. Lassiter rode up front, keeping to himself. Behind, Winters and Murphy were arguing about one of the shots. Handsome Howey was claiming all four kills. The Irishman had killed plenty of men, white and Indian, in his time, and he didn't like the way Winters was carrying on.

"For the love of Jesus," Murphy was saying. "Didn't I see my bullet knock the brains right out of the man's skull? My bullet took that Harpe fella right below the eye."

"Bullshit," Handsome Howey commented.

One thing about these boys, Lassiter thought with sour humor, they got the right spirit.

They split up about two miles from town. Lassiter went in directly by the main trail. Moseley and Murphy circled around so they'd come into town at the other end. Winters and Kingsley spaced out and came in later. Sooner or later, the law would find those five dead buffalo hunters lying out there on the prairie. Lassiter didn't think the law would be interested in the Harpes. Buffalo hunters were always killing or being killed.

He was still some distance from town when he heard the thunder of hooves. It started more like a shaking of the earth than as a sound. The air shook too, a silent shaking at first, then the thunder of a great herd moving began. The thunder grew near and strong until it filled up the whole sky. He reached the end of Texas Street just as the town went wild. That same brass band was playing down by the loading pens. A locomotive whistle tried hard to drown out the band. Six-shooters fired in the air sounded like a small battle. Something like a cannon boomed. Lassiter thought it was a cannon until he recognized the sound as railroad torpedoes being struck with a hammer. It was more than enough noise to start a stampede. Six thousand wild steers wouldn't leave much standing in Abilene if they took it into their bony skulls to go for a run.

Lassiter had been thinking about that for days. He thought it would be one hell of a shame to have a stampede at that particular time. He wanted those six thousand steers ready and waiting when he needed them. If there was any stampeding to be done, he wanted to do it.

Lassiter knew what a cow looked like. He didn't need to see six thousand more. He went upstairs to the room and waited for the others to get back.

Chapter Six

Cassie was waiting for him in his room. Always, after he killed a man, Lassiter found the only way to ease the tension was to put away some whisky or take a woman to bed. Cassie was available and that was better than any bottle. He thought she was available. She would have been if she hadn't been so tensed up. Lassiter said he had a sure cure for that.

Cassie didn't smile. "Is the plan definite now? I'm like to bust if you say no."

"Pretty definite," Lassiter answered. "Unless something happens to change things—we do it tonight."

"There's one change you should know about, Lassiter. Texas Jack has moved into the Drover's Hotel, so Woodruff the cattle buyer can have the parlor car all to himself. Jack wants him to have all the comforts while he's in town.

The pay-off for the cows will begin soon as Woodruff's men count them."

Lassiter didn't see that anything had changed, except now they'd be robbing the cattle buyer instead of Texas Jack. The money was Woodruff's responsibility until the sale went through. That was fine by Lassiter. He was just as ready to rob a man he didn't know as a man he didn't like.

"I guess Texas Jack is just plain lucky," he said to Cassie. "He'll still have his six thousand steers when this is over. If it's any consolation, sis, we'll have to make a mess of his fancy train."

There was bitterness in Cassie's face. "The bastard's got it insured."

Lassiter saw the funny side of it. "Id like to help you put the boots to Jack, but we ain't got the time this trip."

Cassie shrugged. "Forty-five thousand should take some of the edge off. Anyhow, it won't be so easy for Jack to sell his cows once word gets 'round Abilene isn't a safe town for cattle buyers."

Lassiter didn't see it that way. "They can hardly blame Jack. Nobody gets the kind of protection he's giving Woodruff."

A thought came into Lassiter's mind, but he didn't dwell on it. There were thoughts like that before every big job.

Cassie didn't have her brandy bottle along this time. Some of Lassiter's red-eye seemed to make her feel better. She was more like the old raunchy Cassie when she said, "They can brand his butt and sing "Oh, Promise Me," for all I care. As long as I get my share of that money."

"Now you're talking, honey," Lassiter said.

The whisky and the money-talk brought the roses back to Cassie's cheeks. She looked young again, just as greedy. Lassiter didn't mind that. Greedy women were greedy for everything, especially in bed.

"You ever been to San Francisco?" she asked him.

"Not lately."

"Maybe we could go there. What a time we could have."

"Could be," Lassiter agreed.

Cassie's skittishness had passed, and now she was doing her damnedest to make sure he didn't run off with her share of the money. Lassiter hadn't even thought about it. When somebody played square with him, so did he. That was how he worked. Besides, a man with the name of double-crosser didn't last long in his business. Cassie knew that or she wouldn't have sent for him. But like all women, she wanted to be extra sure.

"Get those pants off, Lassiter," she said.

Cassie had always been good in bed. Lassiter couldn't remember any time she was better than now. She used every bed-talent she had to buy extra loyalty. Lassiter was only too happy to lie back and let her persuade him. Cassie was some persuader. He thought he might go with her to Frisco. It would get stale after a week or two, as it did with every woman he had ever known. A man stayed the third week, he started looking for something fresh to chew on. Why the hell not go to Frisco? He was a man of means, with forty-five thousand as good as in the bank. Or at least in his saddlebags.

"Time you got started, sis," he said finally. "We meet as arranged at the farmhouse on the Dillon Road. We can talk about California after the loot is divvied up."

"When do you think you'll get there?" Cassie wanted to know. "Make it quick, will you?"

Pulling on his pants, Lassiter said, "No later than midnight. If we don't make it by twelve, the latest one, we won't be coming."

"So long, Lassiter," Cassie said, putting strength into the goodbye kiss. "We had some good times, didn't we?"

After she left, Lassiter went down the hall to the other room. They were waiting for him. Now that the big job was dead ahead, they were acting more like a team of professionals. Even Murphy and Winters had stopped their cross-talk.

"We been over this before," he began. "Now we go over it again, one step at a time. From Cassie we know the money is in a Salamander safe in Texas Jack's railroad car. The only change is—Jack's moved to the Drover's for the time being. That leaves Woodruff and two guards inside the car. Outside, there are six or eight men with rifles. The parlor car is uncoupled from the locomotive and braked now on the private siding. The caboose with the Gatling gun is standing on another siding, right beside the parlor car. The locomotive's been moved down to the roundhouse."

Lassiter nodded to Kingsley. "Right or wrong?"

"That's how it was fifteen minutes ago," Kingsley answered. "Looks like it stays that way till Woodruff leaves town."

"Maybe," Lassiter said.

He continued: "We could take the six or eight riflemen if that's all there was. Same thing, maybe, for the Gatling. One sure thing—we can't do it cold. So what's the answer."

He looked at Cal Moseley.

Moseley started to talk. "First we start a stampede. I start a stampede. With a help from Juno's firecrackers I get that six thousand cow herd running and point it straight at the depot where the parlor car is. After the cows trample the guards they knock down most of Abilene. That gives us time to do what we came for."

"Maybe," Lassiter said. "You sure the cows ain't heavily guarded."

Cal Moseley grinned, a toothless fox. "Certain," he said. "Just a few punchers. Guess they figure the pens'll hold them."

"Make sure you do it right, Cal," Lassiter warned the old cowman. "We don't get that stampede we don't have a prayer. That whole town'll climb all over us. And it can't be just any old stampede. Them cows got to be right on target."

Old Cal was pissed-off. "I was running off herds before you was born, Lassiter."

Lassiter knew Moseley could do it, if any man could. But there was nothing like a pinch of ginger up the glory hole to make a man bust a gut trying to do better than last time.

The Irishman looked impatient.

"What about the horses?" Lassiter asked him. "You sure you got the right animals?"

T. J. refused to be needled. He knew they still talked about him in the Cavalry as the best horse-handler around. "They're in a boxcar ready to roll soon as Kingsley here provides the transportation. The station agent thinks they're going to Missouri. If you ask me, this is an awful fancy way of doing things. Why can't we just take them animals and ride out of here? All this mucking about with locomotives!"

"I already told you, T. J." Lassiter reminded him. "This ain't just a small town bank we're fixing to rob. Woodruff works for the McCoy Company. Old Joseph McCoy won't sit on his hands once he hears what's happened to his money. Old Joe ain't never been robbed nor bested in a deal. Not yet anyhow. He'll have more rewards on us and more bounty hunters on our tail than the whole James Gang put together. Not to mention every rancher and farmers that owns a weapon. We got to have an edge—and the train gives us that. Gives us a forty mile start and fresh horses."

"Do we have to meet the woman?" Howey Winters complained.

Lassiter ignored him. They'd been over that several times. "What about it?" he asked Kingsley, the trainman. "If you don't think it'll work, say it now. Don't say it later because I won't listen."

Lassiter thought it was funny the way they all came to life when they talked about what they did best. Kingsley was that way now.

"I can do it," he answered. "Right before the stampede we knock out the telegraph going south. Everything's going to be wide open in the wake of that herd. I doubt there'll be many men fretting about railroad property. Man, it'll be a slaughter. All me and Murphy got to do is dress the part, walk in there, and help ourself to Texas Jack's fast locomotive. After that I throw a few switches and couple the car with the horses."

"Then you wait," Lassiter made it plain. "You wait fifteen minutes after the shooting stops. Then you let her roll." He gave Kingsley and the big Irishman a mean grin. " 'Course you can always come and look for us if we don't show up."

"That'll be the day," Murphy said.

Kingsley went on. "Once we get clear of the yards we dynamite the southbound track. The rails out, the wires cut—we have a clear run to the jumping-off place."

"That sounds fine, Oren," Lassiter said. He grinned maliciously. "Now comes the hard part. Here's how it goes. While the rest of you are doing your chores, Flowers, Winters and me go into action. Fifty yards across the tracks from Texas Jack's parlor car is that old stone storehouse. Kingsley here says the railroad kept blasting powder and dynamite there till the town made them move it out. You *are* sure it's empty, ain't you, Kingsley?"

Murphy laughed. "If it wasn't you'd soon find out."

"It's empty," said Kingsley. "People piss in it now."

That seemed definite enough. "The three of us got to be in there before the herd starts running," Lassiter went on. "We can't wait till after. That would give the two men on the Gatling gun—and what was left of the others—too much time to get set again. We have to hit them hard, right in the middle of the stampede. The stone house is where we have to be. Any place else we're stew meat."

"Sounds great," Winters snarled.

"It'll be dark," Lassiter said. "They may spot us. They may not. How the hell do I know. 'Course if anybody's got a better plan."

They didn't have any suggestions. Lassiter didn't think they would.

"It's all suppose," he said. "We suppose they don't spot us. There are two slit windows in the stone house. There was an iron door, but that's gone. Right when the stampede's going good, I open up from one of the windows. That draws their fire in that direction. Winters doesn't start shooting till the flashes tell him where to aim. If Howey doesn't knock out that Gatline—we're dead."

Handsome Howey smirked like the puffed-up little killer he was. A deep crease of annoyance appeared between his colorless eyes when Lassiter said, "If Howey can't do it, me and Flowers will have to start throwing Greek Fire, to light the way. 'Course that could burn up that parlor car too. That's why I don't want to use it."

Lassiter poured himself a small drink. He helped himself to one of the thin cigars in Howey Winters' vest pocket. It tasted sort of sweet, but he stayed with it.

"The Cubans soak those in rum," Winters bragged. "Cost me seventeen dollars a thousand."

"All right," Lassiter continued. "The outside guards are trampled or shot. The cigar expert here has killed or maimed the two men on the Gatling gun. That leaves Woodruff and the two guards inside the parlor car. Woodruff knows the combination to the safe. We try to blow the door open we risk killing him. Flowers could do it fancy so we wouldn't kill him. There isn't time. Besides, them two guards ain't likely to surrender without a fight. They're Texas Jack's men. We got to smoke them out. Make them open the door."

Lassiter said, "Now you can talk, Howey."

The little gun-sharp got up and walked over to his neat, steel-banded trunk. Reaching into it, he took out a box of shells. "This," he said, holding the long, thick bullet between thumb and forefinger, "is the biggest shell made anywhere." Winters sounded like a professor in a school for killers. "It's three and a quarter inches long. It's got seven hundred grains of lead and a hundred and seventy grains of powder."

"Christ Almighty," the Irishman declared.

Winters was showing off. Lassiter let him do

it. He didn't care what else the little killer did as long as he did the job he was hired for.

"And here's the little beauty that throws such a slug," Winters said, bending again and coming up with a blanket-coddled weapon. "This is a .54-caliber Sharps and if you don't think it'll shoot through Bismarck glass, you're loco, and so's your mother. If it doesn't do it the first time, it sure as shooting will do it the second."

Murphy knew something about guns and the new bullet-proof glass they had invented in Germany to keep their kings and princes from getting kiboshed by anarchists and other head-cases. "You shot through Bismarck glass, have you, Howey?" T. J. enquired.

Winters gloated. "The Army done it with a Sharps just like this," he said. "That was back in Washington two years ago. You ought to read more, Murph."

Lassiter took over again. "Now there ain't no more Bismarck glass—we suppose. The doors are still locked from the inside. We can't climb through the window over broken glass with two guards shooting at us."

Juno Flowers, usually with nothing to say, was ahead of him. The gloomy explosives-lover said, "We smoke them out. Or stink them out or both. Sliced-up celluloid collars wrapped in wet felt with a fast fuse running through makes the best smoke bomb you ever saw. The celluloid wants to burn like mad, but the wet felt won't let it. You get the foulest smoke short of a burn-ing skunk—and plenty of it."

"And we throw in more than one so they get

the idea," Lassiter said. "Flowers says it works faster'n we can talk about it. They won't have much fight left when they do—Flowers says. Woodruff less than that, I guess. We ask him nice to open the safe. If he doesn't, we kill him. We hope he'll see the sensible side of it. If not, Flowers will blow the safe with nitro . . ."

"And off we go," Howey Winters chimed in.

Lassiter had broken his left arm some years back. Sometimes it hurt. It hurt now. He rubbed it. "Maybe," he said. "It's all a maybe."

The Irishman heaved his huge frame out of the ruined wicker chair and stretched his legs. He rubbed his doggy nose and yawned. "By Jesus," he announced, "I ain't had that much instructin' since I was a boy at school."

Howey Winters held up a can of gun oil and shook it. "What school, T. J.?" he sneered.

Lassiter stepped between them. "Ladies," he informed them, "that was just a fast rehearsal, as the traveling players say. "Now we take it slow and easy. Kingsley, you got a conductor's watch. Timing, they tell me, is goddamned important."

Lassiter's smile was so warm it would have hatched an alligator egg.

"Mother of God," Murphy said.

Chapter Seven

Abilene was still celebrating the arrival of Texas Jack's big herd. With Texas Jack's first few rounds of free drinks to get it started, the town was still spending its own money to get drunk. The saloons were doing a land office business. Lights blazed up and down the main stretch of Texas Street. Upstairs over the saloons the whores hadn't been off their backs since morning, except to eat a little to keep up their strength. During the long, wild afternoon one of Texas Jack's boys shot and killed the old colored daddy who swamped out the Alamo Saloon. The sheriff locked him up and said he'd get fined good for that. The sheriff was sick of Texans. He didn't know when he'd been so busy.

At eight-thirty, Moseley, Kingsley and Murphy drifted down toward the railroad yards. Moseley went by himself. Lassiter thought it was kind of funny to see the old stock-thief with his pockets stuffed with Chinese firecrackers. Kingsley and Murphy carried rolled-up denim coats and hats. When they got to the quiet end of Texas Street, by the railroad yards, they put them on. It was dark and quiet in the yards and they moved confidently like men who knew where they were going.

Winters and Juno Flowers went next, at eight-forty. Handsome Howey complained about having to leave his gun trunk behind. Now he carried the blanket-wrapped weapons, the big Sharps with the shortened barrel and the Remington-Schuetzen, in an oilskin cover. Walking slowly, Flowers carried the explosives in a black bag. In their city clothes they looked like a drummer and maybe a horse doctor on their way to the depot. Abilene was full of strangers—gamblers, salesmen, reporters, sky-pilots, speculaross, shysters—and nobody paid Winters and Flowers the slightest heed.

Some distance behind, Lassiter watched them disappear into the half-darkness of the yards. He walked the rest of the way slowly, giving them time to get set. On the way he stopped to roll a smoke, but he didn't light it. Only the usual sounds came from the yards. A locomotive letting loose steam. The clanging of a bell. Dodging the light from the oil lanterns hung here and there, he waited for a string of freight cars to pass between the old stone storehouse and the men guarding the parlor car fifty yards on the other side of the tracks. When the freight cars passed he was inside the stone building.

The Winchester was hanging inside his coat on a rawhide thong. He took the coat off and threw it in a corner.

Some of the dim light from the yards found its way inside the building. "Jesus, this place stinks," Winters said. The little killer had unwrapped his weapons and was standing back from one of the slit windows, sighting on the parlor car and caboose across the way.

Lassiter took up his position at the other window. "What about it?" he asked. "How does it look from here?"

"It's all right," Winters answered. "I just want to get this thing over and out of here. What a frigging stink!"

Lassiter watched the guards standing in front of the parlor car. There were eight of them. He figured they would be piss-burned because they had to watch over that goddamned money while the rest of the town was getting drunk. That was all to the good. It could make them careless.

The windows of the parlor car were all lit up. The shades were pulled down. The cattle buyer was spending a quiet evening at home. Or so he thought. The freight that had gone into the yards five minutes before started to come out again. Lassiter cursed silently when it stopped right in front of them. He didn't know why it stopped there. They listened tensely while the engineer swore at the fireman. Lassiter felt his dry, hard hands gripping the Winchester. There wasn't a thing they could do. At the other window Winters were shaking with agner. "Sweet Jesus," he whispered over and over. Lassiter knew how the little bastard felt. Less than five minutes from now Cal Moseley would start the herd running.

"They spoil this I'll kill them both," Winters snarled. Lassiter told him to shut up. Just then the door of the depot office banged open and the station agent yelled at the engineer to get that dad-blamed train out of there. Lassiter's breath came out slowly. He shouldered the Winchester and sighted in again.

Winters was doing the same thing. Holding his bag of tricks, Juno Flowers stood with his back against the wall. The safe-blower wasn't nervous any longer. Beyond the yards the huge penned-up herd bawled in the darkness.

The first string of firecrackers went off. Then the second, then the third. Then there was some shooting as Cal Moseley cut down on the cow-pucnhers watching the longhorns. A sound like a huge groan swept through the herd and the ground started to shake as thousands of tons of cowflesh began to move. The firecrackers started again and the thunder grew loud. One of the guards in front of the parlor car yelled something. Suddenly the cow pens burst wide open and six thousand fear-crazed longhorns were headed right for the depot. Goodbye, town, Lassiter thought.

Like a fast-flowing river, the huge herd swept over the railroad yards. A river in full flood, it spread out, thickened and picked up speed, wrecking and tearing apart everything in its way. At first the guards in front of the parlor car were confused about what to do. By the time they decided to run it was too late. Lassiter chewed on a dry cigarette and watched the herd sweep over them. He listened to their screams and thought about the money. Maybe he would go to Frisco with Cassie. Maybe not.

The stone building was like a lighthouse in the middle of a storm. The flood of bawling cows swept by the open door. Across the way it boiled up around the parlor car and the caboose where the Gatling gun was. The heavy cars held steady. The shades on the parlor car windows snapped up. Lassiter could see the fat bulk of the frightened cattle buyer and the two guards. "Now," he said to Winters.

Lassiter levered fast and fired fast. Just as he fired the last shot, the Gatling gun started to chatter. A line of bullets stitched the wall as he ducked back and started to reload. The Gatling stopped and started again. This time some of the bullets came through the door, flattening against the back wall. All it would take was one ricochet to blow them sky high. Juno's bag had enough nitro and stick-dynamite to do that. "You got it yet, Howey?" Lassiter asked.

"In a minute, for Christ's sake," Winters snarled, sighting the big rifle. "Shoot some more."

Across the way, while the longhorns thundered on through, Lassiter saw one of the outside guards crawling up the steps of the parlor car. The man was pounding on the heavy steel-lined door. It didn't open. Lassiter saw no reason to waste a bullet just to draw the Gatling's fire. He shot the man, knocking him clear off the steps.

The Gatling answered right away. Out of the way, he heard Winters say, "Strut your stuff, baby." The Gatling was still spraying the slit window where Lassiter was when Winters fired. There was a scream and the revolving barrel of the rapid-fire gun stopped winking. It started again a moment later. The second gunner was scared. This time he hardly aimed the gun at all. He ran through a whole strip of bullets, firing as fast as he could turn the crank, spraying everything in sight with hot lead. Winters sighted again and fired. The Gatling stopped firing.

"Time to go, Juno," Lassiter told Flowers. If there had been time Lassiter would have tested the Gatling some more. There wasn't. The man behind the Gatling might not be dead, might not even be wounded. He might be sitting there in the dark, behind the gun, waiting for a better chance.

The tail end of the stampede was out of the yards now. A few strays ran around bawling. Now it was the town's turn to learn how fast six thousand cows could run, how much damage they could do. Lassiter and Flowers started across the turn-up yards at a crouching run. They got as far as the tracks when the Gatling started firing again. Bullets ripped and tore all around them. "God, I'm hit," Flowers gasped. Behind them Lassiter heard Winters firing fast. The Gatling stopped again.

"How bad is it?" Lassiter asked, supporting

the wounded man as they stumbled across the tracks.

"I don't know," Flowers said, wheezing. "I think I can make it."

Down past the yards the town was coming parat. A building began to burn. The lights in the parlor car had gone out. Winters was firing again, this time with the huge single-shot Sharps. The first big shell crashed against the Bismarck glass. Keeping low, Lassiter and Flowers kept going. The big Sharps fired again. The heavy bullet didn't ricochet, but it didn't go through. Lassiter cursed Winters and his goddamned guns. Lassiter knew Winters could load and fire faster than that. But he knew the gunsharp was trying to put them all in the same place. The Sharps boomed again and the thick window burst wide open.

The two men inside the car started shooting through the jagged hole in the glaass. Changing back to the fast-fire Remington, Winters sent them ducking for cover. That gave Lassiter just enough time to drag Flowers alongside the parlor car. Flowers was hurt bad all right. Lassiter had to pull hard to pry the black bag loose from his hand. Opening, he felt the wet-felt smoke bombs, the shredded celluloid inside, the fuse sticking out at the end.

Winters stopped firing to reload. One of the guards fired as Lassiter lit the first fuse and stood up to throw it. He felt the breeze of the bullet. From across the yards, Winters fired again. The guard's body hit the floor of the car with a crash. Every time Lassiter threw a smoke bomb Winters fired. One of the bombs hit the glass and bounced into the yard. Lassiter threw the last bomb and dragged Flowers underneath the car.

"I'll be back," he said.

Flowers nodded weakly.

Lassiter crawled along under the car. Thick oily smoke was pouring from the wrecked window. He crawled until he reached the teps. Winters ran across the tracks carrying the two heavy rifles. Inside the car Lassiter could hear choking and coughing. Winters dropped on one knee and put three fast shots through the window. Lassiter inched up the steps of the parlor car and beat on the door. "Open up," he yelled. "You won't get another chance. Be smart, Woodruff."

Thirty seconds dragged by. Lassiter told them again. "All right! All right!" a voice said.

Lassiter swung out of the way. The door opened with a crash and the smoke rushed out. The second guard came out after it. He came out too fast, with a gun in his hand. Lassiter shot him dead. "Show yourself, Woodruff," he yelled.

The cattle buyer's jowly face showed white through the black smoke. Lassiter told him to keep his hands up. Woodruff whined when Lassiter pushed him back inside the car. Winters followed and took up his position at the window. Lassiter fanned out the worst of the smoke and touched a match to one of the gas-lights. The dead guard on the floor looked as if somebody had split his head with an axe. Winters looked at him with professional interest.

Lassiter dug the muzzle of his Colt into Woodruff's belly. "Open it," he ordered.

"You'll kill me anyway," the cattle buyer whined.

"Maybe," Lassiter said. "Now open it."

"Look at that town burn," Winters said at the window.

Grunting, the cattle buyer knelt in front of the safe. Lassiter had to prod him again before his fat fingers started to twist the dial. The tumblers clicked, then the fat man made a mistake and had to begin again. Sweat poured down the back of his fat neck. Then finally, the heavy door swung open. Lassiter shoved him out of the way. He reached into the safe and Winters' big rifle boomed heavily in the enclosed space. Lassiter's gun came out fast, hammer back. The fat man was sagging to the floor with a huge hole in his belly. He still had his hand under his coat.

Winters grinned. "You're getting careless, Lassiter," the little killer said. "Woodruff knew we'd kill him. He had to try something."

"You start packing the money," Lassiter said. "I got to see to Flowers."

"That's mighty trusting of you, Lassiter."

"What do you think?"

Winters carried the sack of money. Lassiter carried Flowers. A man appeared from behind a freight car and fired at them. Lassiter dodged and Winters fired the long-barreled .32 with his left hand. The man died with a bullet in his head.

By now the town knew something was up, not just a stampede. With the wounded man across his shoulder, Lassiter wheeled about and saw men running from the end of Texas Street. Down by the roundhouse, Kingsley was backing the engine up to the boxcar where the horses were. Winters and Lassiter broke into a dead run. The heavy coupling links clanged as Kingsley secured the horse-car.

Murphy leaned out of the cab and roared at them to get a move on. There was blood on the back of the big Irishman's denim coat. Old Cal Moseley was already in the boxcar with the horses. Winters heaved the sack of money into the car and climbed in after it. Lassiter pitched Juno Flowers in after it. Then he was on board too.

"Did you get it, boss? Did you get it?" the Irishman roared from up front. He ducked in his head as a rifle bullet whanged off the side of the cab. Other shots sounded as men poured into the yards. The town of Abilene was good and mad. Old Cal Moseley fingered his twisted neck.

"Move it! Oh, Christ, move it!" Winters howled.

Chapter Eight

There was a blast of white-hot steam as Kingsley eased up the throttle. Metal screamed. Dragging no weight, the powerful Mogul locomotive spun its wheels, throwing sparks. The big driving wheels began to turn, slowly at first, then Kingsley released more power. The train started to roll.

A minute later it was rolling fast. The big headlight up front sliced through the darkness. Murphy had a hole under the right shoulder. He yanked a quart bottle of whisky out of his coat pocket and broke the neck on the side of the cab. This time he wasn't showing off. There wasn't time to do anything.

The Irishman didn't know how bad he was hurt. The pain was bad enough. Frothy blood appeared at the corners of his mouth when he gagged on the whisky. He let out a yell that

Lassiter could hear back in the boxcar. The Irishman was crazy all right. Kicking open the firebox, he started to sing some wild tune, bending and heaving, pitching wood.

Bullets thudded into the back of the boxcar. Lassiter stuck his head out the side door and looked back. One side of Texas Street was burning. He could hear the bell on the steam fire engine clanging. A stray bullet zipped past his face like an angry bee.

Cal Moseley was trying to quiet the horses. Up front Kingsley was putting the big engine through its paces. The noise and the shooting faded behind them. Lassiter braced himself against the roll of the car. He lit the swinging oil lamp. The thin yellow light showed Juno Flowers lying on his back on a pile of hay, just where they'd thrown him.

Winters was more worried about his guns. When he saw how bad Flowers was, he had an idea. "Is he dead?" he asked Lassiter.

Lassiter felt the side of Flowers' neck. There was a fast, weak pulse. Lassiter ripped open the dying man's shirt and felt his heart. It fluttered and skipped under his fingers. "Not yet," he said. "He won't last long."

Winters was thinking about the dying man's share of the money. But even he didn't want to come right out and talk about it. "Poor bastard," the little killer said. He was a rotten actor. "Better put him out of his misery. Nothing else we can do."

Lassiter looked at him. "He's got an hour to die, Howey. Let him do it his own way."

A shower of sparks blazed past the open door of the boxcar. Winters was hanging on to the stretch rope that kept the horses in line. "I'll do it, Lassiter," he said, taking the long-barreled .32 from under his coat.

Lassiter had his feet wide apart to steady himself. His hands hung loose and relaxed. "Put away that gun," he warned Winters. "Or I'll put you away."

The sack of money lay on the floor between them. Winters looked at it and laughed. "Sure, Lassiter," he said. "No call for us to quarrel."

There was a band of tension around Lassiter's head. It grew tighter, like drying rawhide. Now that the job was done he wanted to get his share of the money. He just wanted to get away from there, from Winters, from all of them. People, any kind of people, got on his nerves after a while. The same with towns and saloons and too much talk and noise.

"Sure, Howey," he said. There was still about thirty minutes to go, he figured. He sat down beside the dying man on the heaped-up hay and drank from a bottle. Whisky, even tobacco, always tasted bitter when the tension was in his head. He drank some more whisky. He didn't offer any to Moseley or Winters.

Winters unwrapped his two rifles from the blanket and rubbed them with an oily rag. The big rifles gleamed dully in the yellow light. A trailing spark flew in the door and landed on Lassiter's boot. He poured some whisky on it. Unlike most men, he didn't get strung-out and talky when the danger was past. Men like that gave him a pain the the sit-spot. The tension in his head never showed, not unless you knew him well. And nobody did.

Up front, Murphy was slinging more wood. Every time he did, there was a roar and a glare. It stopped when he kicked the door shut. The bottle was half gone. Lassiter could tell time by inches of whiskey in a bottle. About fifteen minutes now.

Juno Flowers began to mumble. Lassiter had seen a lot of men die. The ones who talked too much in life usually died without saying anything. The quiet ones, like Flowers, seemed to want to make up for lost time. Flowers thought he was back in the Civil War. Flowers had fought for the South. "A pleasure and an honor," he mumbled.

Lassiter didn't know what he'd do about Cassie. It didn't make a hell of a lot of difference, one way or the other. Maybe he'd take his forty-five thousand and ride down to El Paso. The girls in Betsy Shannock's fancy whorehouse didn't talk unless you wanted them to.

The locomotive bell clanged and the train started to lose speed. The bottle was finished and Lassiter stood up. Air brakes hissed and the train dragged to a halt. It looked like everything was working out just fine. Winters was no good with horses. Lassiter told him to stay the hell out of the way. Murphy stumbled along the side of the train with a lantern and told Moseley to start sending down the horses.

Then the horses were down and they were ready to go. The money was tied across the front of Lassiter's saddle. They all kept looking at it. Lassiter was the last to leave the boxcar. The dying man was still talking. Holding the oil lamp in one hand, Lassiter drew his gun with the other. Juno Flowers opened his eyes. Lassiter couldn't tell if he knew him. He shot Flowers twice through the head.

Still holding the lamp, he jumped down. Kingsley's face was stuck out the side of the engine cab. "Okay?" he asked. Lassiter nodded and threw the lamp into the boxcar. It smashed and the hay caught. Kingsley pulled down the throttle and tied it. The train was moving when he jumped down.

The blazing train rocketed into the darkness. Long streamers of flame stretched out behind it. After the glare it was hard to see for a while. By the time their eyes got used to darkness again the train was a mile away. They all stayed close to Lassiter. The Irishman was swaying in his saddle, but he kept going. They had just picked up the narrow trail called Dillon Road when there was a bright flash and a bombing sound in the distance.

"That was a right nice locomotive," Oren Kingsley commented, riding heavily like a man out of his element. Juno Flowers wasn't mentioned.

After they'd been riding for a while, Moseley asked, "How much longer?"

Lassiter said about an hour. The farmhouse where they were to meet Cassie had been abandoned for years. They couldn't miss it, she said. It was the first house they'd come to after the railroad. There wasn't another house for miles. They would stay there long enough to count the money and divvy it up. It was all in large bills and wouldn't take long. It was mighty considerate of Mr. Woodruff to arrange it like that. One thing Lassiter hated about robbing small town banks—it took so long to count the small stuff. Mostly, when he worked alone and there was no divvy, he didn't bother. It didn't last any longer if you knew how much it was. How long would the forty-five thousand last?

Murphy had trouble staying aboard his animal. Lassiter wondered if he'd have to kill him. They couldn't leave him to be caught by bounty hunters and company detectives. He had once seen a man after company detectives got through with him. Every part of his body was black with cigar burns, even the soles of his feet. Lassiter grinned. That was the humane side of it. Everybody who'd seen them pulling the robbery was dead and, with luck or something, they might never be identified. Not for sure anyway. The Irishman could spoil that.

A weak light winked up ahead. With the divvy just minutes away, Winters got excited and spurred his horse. "St. Louie here I come," he said. Lassiter told him to shut up and ride easy.

They could see the shape of the house now, low and squat, set back from the trail in a grove of trees. Part of the roof looked to have fallen in. When they got closer, Lassiter could see the light was a short candle guttering inside a broken window.

"Space out," he told them. He drew his Colt and spun the chamber. There wasn't a sound except the horses thudding in the thick dust. The shape of the house got bigger and they rode on through, past a rotting farm wagon. Nothing happened.

"Aw come on," Winters complained. "What's all this pussyfooting for. Let's split up the money and take off." He got down off his horse before he was told. The Irishman fell off his, cursing and laughing. Moseley and Oren Kingsley waited for Lassiter to make his move.

It looked all right and he was starting to get down when the short hairs prickled on the back of his neck. There was a smell. The smell did it. It was the smell of coal oil. He swing back into the saddle as guns blazed and cracked from three sides. A match flared and Lassiter killed the man holding it. The man dropped and the match went out. Then there was another match and a cut-down barrel of coal oil flamed high in the darkness. A bullet burned a shallow crease along Lassiter's ribs. Another took the hat off his head. He emptied his six-shooter at the gun flashes nearest him. A man screamed. Lassiter holstered his gun and yanked the Winchester free of the scabbard. Another bullet took splinters out of the stock, almost knocked the rifle out of his hand. Trying to turn the horse, he levered and fired.

Murphy was up on his feet, shooting with both hands. A rain of bullets slammed into his thick body, but he didn't go down. Cornered, Winters was screaming like the rat he was. His horse bucked and plunged as he tried to climb into the saddle. Winters knew he was going to die. That gave him rat courage. Dodging and twisting, he stayed on his feet for more than ten seconds. A shotgun boomed and Howey Winters lost his head.

Murphy lurched and stumbled with empty guns in his hands. Then a rifle bullet tore away the side of his skull and he fell like a tree. Lassiter wheeled his horse around as Oren Kingsley dropped from his saddle. They got Kingsley's horse too. Cal Moseley was already dead. Lassiter felt his horse jerk as a bullet sliced through its neck. The dying animal started to run. Lead nicked the tip of Lassiter's left ear. The blood felt hot and greasy on his neck. One-handing the rifle, he pegged a quick shot at the blazing barrel of coal oil. It blew up and the house started to burn. The dying horse took Lassiter out of there. A man dressed in black ran into the circle of light and fired at him. Lassiter couldn't make him out. He missed though. Lassiter's horse died and dropped, throwing him. There wasn't time to think about the money sack lashed to the front of the saddle. They were coming after him now. Bullets whacked into the dead horse and scattered the dust. Lassiter grabbed up the rifle and ran.

Out in the darkness the ambushers weren't so brave. Lassiter vaulted a split-rail fence and crouched down behind it. He thumbed a load of shells into the Winchester and waited, breathing hard. A shower of burning brands exploded into the night sky as the gutted farmhouse collapsed.

That was the last light there was. Outlined against it he saw the shapes of men and horses. About ten of both, he figured. He still couldn't make them out. Two of the eager ones started to ride after him. He dropped both of them and started running again.

He knew he didn't have a chance, but he kept on going. Dark or not, they could run him down on the open prairie. Or they could wait till sunup and run him down the easy way. A man on foot couldn't get very far. Without a horse, without water, he was a soft target.

Flat in the waving prairie grass, he waited and listened. He cursed softly when he heard them riding away. He waited some more, thinking it was a trick. They might be riding out wide, hoping to take him from all sides. While he waited the sound of the horses died away. The wind came up and it was cold on the prairie.

Lassiter rubbed his hands together, trying to stay warm while he figured a few things out. Those few things had got kind of complicated. It looked that way from where he was now. It smelled like a doublecross, but since he didn't know for sure, he didn't decide about Cassie. The others were all dead. It wasn't any of them. Only a fool would set up an ambush and then ride into it himself. He thought of Winters, Murphy, Kingsley, and Moseley, now being packed back to Abilene.

There were several explanations that came to mind. Cassie might have set it up. If she hadn't, then who in the hell were the ambushers? Lassiter stopped thinking about it. Nothing wore out a man faster than having his mind go 'round in circles, like a pup chasing its tail. One thing was damn sure—he was going to have a little talk with Cassie.

Two coyotes began a duet. Lassiter waited and listened. After the best part of two hours he got up and stretched his cramped legs. Abilene was more than forty miles that way. He started back for the burned-out farmhouse. Some of them might still be there, waiting. They might have ridden off a ways, then come back on foot. He started back anyway, rifle at the ready.

He vaulted over the split-rail fence. Red coals glowed in the darkness. That was all that was left of the house. The dead horse was the first thing he came to. They had taken the saddle but left the rest of his gear. Poking about, he found the canteen, still full. After he drank he wet his bandana and wiped the dried blood off his neck. The nicked earlobe was swollen, and ached with dull pain. The crease along his ribs was nothing more than that. The bullet hadn't even touched the bones. It was more like a burn than a wound.

He cocked the rifle when he heard a sound out behind the ruins of the house. The smell of coal oil was still strong. He relaxed and set down the hammer of the Winchester when he saw it was a horse still saddled, Cal Moseley's animal. The horse was skittish and Lassiter thought of that forty mile walk between him and Abilene. "Easy boy," he said.

Lassiter stayed still and spoke horse-talk. When he tried to edge forward the animal backed away, shaking its head and pawing the ground. He shook the canteen and talked soft to the animal. It whinnied at the sound of water. Lassiter unstoppered the canteen and poured a trickle of water into his hat. He did it slowly, coaxing the scary animal. He poured a little more water, splashing it thin and high. This time he didn't move. He let the animal come to him.

Well now, Lassiter thought, that wasn't so bad. Things were beginning to look up. He didn't know if he would get another crack at that bale of money. Money or no money, there were questions had to be asked—and answered —before he decided what to do next. Losing the money was one of those things a man had to expect in the sort of business he was in. There would be other cattle drives, other payrolls, other gold shipments, other banks. Losing the money, by itself, didn't cause him any grief. If it was a plain case of bad luck—say those ambushers were stray local law or bounty hunters that happened along-well, then, he'd just have to take it that way. Getting shot up by the law was nothing to take personally. But if Cassie— or someone—had brought him all the way to Kansas to use as a goat, that was altogether different. That made it personal. Lassiter was a professional—he admired a smart doublecross —but a man had to do something about it, if that's what it was. A man couldn't let them sit back and figure him for a fool.

Mounting up, he started back for Abilene.

Chapter Nine

He crossed the railroad after following the
Dillon Road back from the farmhouse. The telegraph wires hummed in the darkness. There was
no other sound. He walked the horse across the
right of way to where the old trail picked up on
the other side. A mile from there he got back on
the main trail going north to Abilene.

Once, he ducked his horse behind a scatter of
rocks and held its nose when a group of horsemen rode by. They were traveling fast, even in
the dark, and Lassiter would have bet money
they were looking for him and the others. They
didn't look to be the same bunch that had done
the ambushing. This bunch were riding too close
and making too much noise to be professional
manhunters. Most likely they were farmers or
small ranchers with pictures of big reward
money in their heads.

Traveling cautious, Lassiter made twenty miles before first light. This was settled farming country, most of it, not a bit like the vast sun-blasted deserts of Arizona and New Mexico, where a man could go for days without seeing another human being, hostile or friendly. Kansas didn't suit him much and he'd be glad when he could turn his mount and head back south.

He made cold camp just as the sun was coming up. Tired and hungry, he would have settled for a long hard drink of whisky. There was nothing to eat in Moseley's saddle bags, and nothing to drink. A search turned up nothing but a hunk of black chewing tobacco. It was better than nothing and he worked on that for a bit, huddled in the dead man's blanket roll in the shade of a cottonwood cluster beside a muddy creek.

The black flies gave him some trouble at first. They went away when the sun came up full. He wondered if Abilene knew him by name and description. If Cassie—or someone—had staged that ambush, knowing they were coming, it was dead certain they knew who he was. That made the whole thing kind of chancy. Everything sure as hell pointed to Cassie, but Lassiter never jumped the gun about anything, just as he never took anything for granted.

He had known Cassie a lot of years. They'd been through good and bad times together. They went back a long way, and that should count for something, but Lassiter knew better than tthat. People got older and sometimes that changed them. It wasn't anything to fret about.

It was a fact, something that happened, like the sun coming up every morning. Cassie had always been a greedy little bitch. So was he, in a different sort of way. Money—well, no, the getting of money and the spending of it was what he lived for. But that hadn't turned him into a doublecrosser and back-shooter. People were all the same, he guessed, and they were all different. If Cassie had set up this double-cross, she would have to be reminded that he hadn't changed. Having yourself killed was a drastic way to be reminded of something. Lassiter wasn't all that keen on killing Cassie, doublecrosser or not—what else could he do? Cassie was no amateur. She knew the rules about as well as he did. It was a high stakes game. When you lost, you lost big. There wasn't anything bigger than losing your life.

Lassiter slept for three hours and when he woke up he knew he was going into Abilene by daylight. There was one edge he had—they wouldn't be looking for him in a town he'd recently robbed and wrecked. They might not hang him for robbing the cattle buyer. They sure as shooting would string him up for wrecking the town. Lassiter didn't mean to give them the chance to decide.

Lassiter rooted through old Cal's warbag and came up with something like a change of duds. The old stock-thief had been living a town life in recent years, but he still toted around some go-to-meeting clothes in his warbag. Or maybe he'd never taken them out of there. They smelled that way to Lassiter, musty and too long without a breath of fresh air. There was a more or less clean white shirt, a badly folded black frock coat, and a shapeless black wool hat without band or lining. Digging deep, Lassiter found a crumpled, stand-up paper collar and a patent leather cravat.

He tried fitting the paper collar to the smudgy linen shirt. Lassiter was lean but old Cal had been hunger-thin, and it wouldn't work. The out-of-date frock coat was long enough and fit pretty good, except for strain across the shoulders and some bunching under the arms. Lassiter hated to put on that goddamned wool hat. It made him feel—and look, he guessed— like a fool. Well I'll be damned, he thought when he stuffed his own hat into the dead stock-thief's warbag and found a pair of badly bent spectacles.

He tried on old Cal's hideaway glasses and couldn't see a thing. It looked as if Cal had been closer to the rocking chair age than he'd figured. He wondered why Cal Moseley had any kind of glasses, since the old buzzard hadn't been able to read or write his own name. Lassiter slid the steel-rimmed glasses down on his nose and, feeling foolish, bent his shoulders in an old man's hump. Without a mirror, he didn't know if he looked like an unfrocked preacher, a snake oil pedlar, or an unburied corpse.

It would do fine, he decided, though he wasn't happy about the possibility of being killed in an outfit like that. Lassiter's reputation was the last thing he worried about, but to have his picture in the *Abilene-Sentinel* in such a get-up would be a bad end to any man's life.

The sun said it was all of two o'clock when he got near Abilene. More than ever he needed a drink of whisky. More than that, he wanted to feel his hands around Cassie McCord's neck while she explained or failed to explain exactly why a near-perfect robbery had turned sour just when it was time to split the take and start smiling. Naturally, he was ready to learn that Cassie had left town in a hurry. He was ready for that, but he didn't think so. He had a hunch that it had started in Abilene, and would end there.

Lassiter was no actor and he didn't try to be. He'd just as soon they hanged him as try to pretend to be something or somebody he wasn't. He wondered if the horse would give him away, even if the Sunday duds got him through this thing unnoticed. It was a goddamned fine animal, much too good for the shabby old fraud he looked like now, that he hoped he looked like now.

The road into town passed by the railroad yards. There was no doubt that the taking of Mathew Woodruff's money was the biggest event Abilene had worried about since the drought of '73.

They hadn't got all of Texas Jack's six thousand cows back in the pens yet. Lassiter rode by at a canter, four-eyed under the droopy hat, bent in the saddle, coattails flapping in the breeze he stirred up. Fourteen hours had gone by since the taking of the cattle buyer's money.

As far as Abilene was concerned it was still new news.

There was the parlor car just as they had left it, with the big hole Howey Winters had punched in the Bismarck-glassed window with the Sharps. The caboose was there too, looking no different. A man standing behind a camera on a tripod with a black cloth over his head was telling the sightseers to get out of the way. The sightseers were yelling back, telling the photographer to take their picture too, or to go to hell. As Lassiter rode by, the colonel with the burnside whiskers came out of the wrecked parlor car shaking his head.

It was still too recent for the company detectives to be there. Lassiter saw the thick-set sheriff, flanked by three of his deputies. The sheriff looked at Lassiter as he rode into town past the yards. Lassiter wasn't slighted by the sheriff's lack of interest. He liked it. He didn't think he could have acted the character that went with the clothes, if the sheriff had been interested enough to ask his name, and his business in Abilene.

Lassiter started along Texas Street. Now he knew how a town looked after six thousand longhorns had run over it. It hadn't been much of a town anyway. The stampede must have killed more than the gunmen guarding the train. That didn't bother Lassiter. People were born to die, and a nice quick stampede was every bit as good as blackwater fever, or lung fever, or brain fever, or a knot in the guts, or a cancer of the heart.

One whole side of Texas Street was knocked down, part by fire, part by running cows. The Thompson Hotel where Cassie lived, or had lived, was still standing. The porch had been partly swept away, but the hotel was built of brick, the only hotel in town so built, and it looked like a hotel that needed only a fine front porch to make it look right.

Past that was The Pearl, a saloon Lassiter had never been in. He went there now, to have the drink of whisky he'd been thinking about since the sack of money had turned up missing. If Cassie was at the Thompson Hotel, she could wait a while longer. If not, she could wait a while longer.

Lassiter knew he was a rotten actor. He tried anyway, trying to remember how he must have sounded when he spoke when he first came west. "Didn't know they had cyclones this time of year," he said to the bartender in The Pearl who drew his beer, then poured his whisky.

"Cyclone," said the drink-pourer. "You must be new in town, old-timer." The bartender sounded proud. "How many towns you seen can take a stampede of six thousand cows and pour you a drink the morning after? Not to mention the biggest robbery in the history of the state. By cracky, wouldn't I like to have some of that money. They got the whole bunch except the one with the money. That fella got clean away. Three hundred and eighty thousand is what that fella got. Think about it, old-timer—three hundred-eighty thousand dollars! Ain't that something to think about."

"The Lord's business is more important, but a heap of money it is," Lassiter said to the barkeep. "Think of the tabernacle could be raised with such a sum? 'Twould make the Saints of Utah hang they heads in shame."

The barkeep set down the bottle in front of Lassiter. "Texas Jack's boys got all of them but the one with the money." The bottle custodian was as excited as if the money had been his own. "They packed them back to town this morning but nary a smell of the money did they have."

Cassie? Texas Jack? Lassiter lingered on his second drink of whisky. There was no harm in asking, not with the bartender sounding off the way he was. "Must be a right smart fella, God forgive his avarice, not only robbing such a sum but getting away with it."

"By George," Lassiter said, shaking his head. "Have a drink or a cigar or something, barkeep. Usually I don't hold with smoking, but, now, ain't that something!"

The bartender said he didn't smoke. Didn't smoke usually, like the man said, but, well, he'd have a drink, it being such a special occasion and all.

Lassiter raised his glass as the bartender drank his own poison. The barkeep bought Lassiter a drink and they mulled over the robbery.

"Who is this fella anyway?" Lassiter asked. "You sure it ain't Jesse James?"

"It's Lassiter," the barkeep said. "A fella goes by the name of Lassiter. You ever hear of him, 'cause I ain't?"

"No," Lassiter said, thinking some. "But a name don't mean much. "I say it's the James boys and you can say what you like. There was talk of the Quantrills some days back, and you know them James fellas and the Colonel's son is thicker than thieves."

Lassiter corrected himself. "Least as thick. As thieves, I mean to say."

"You want another?" the barkeep asked.

The barkeep poured. He winked at Lassiter. Lassiter winked back. Lassiter's spectacles kept slipping and he adjusted them again. The barkeep poured himself a drink and put it away fast.

"Forget about the James boys," the bartender said solemnly. "This was done by a fella name of Lassiter. A real hard-case from down south. They got men all over looking for him right now."

Lassiter signaled for another drink. "They ain't a-going to catch Jesse," he said.

"It's Lassiter, for Christ' sake," the barkeep said. "And he ain't about to get away with it. Ain't a man alive can get away with four hundred eighty thousand dollars."

"How much?" Lassiter asked.

"More than that," the barkeep said.

Lassiter had to pass the sheriff's office and jail to get to the Thompson Hotel. He couldn't say it wasn't interesting. One deputy was nailing up a wanted poster for a robber named Lassiter while two others were setting his four friends out to take the air on an undertaker's cooling boards. Of course, Kingsley, Murphy, Moseley, and Winters had cooled some time ago. Now they were stiff as the boards they were lying on.

The same photographer was trying to take pictures, and was having the same problems. Stopping to look at his four departed associates, Lassiter wondered if some day he would end up on a cooling board like that. So many hard-cases had, and did, and would.

At the Thompson Hotel he asked the day clerk if Miss McCord was up yet. Cassie never did like to get up early, then, or, he guessed, now. Lassiter wondered how Texas Jack was taking all the excitement.

The elderly room clerk frowned at Lassiter. "Miss McCord has been up for some time," he said. "She's having breakfast now."

Lassiter looked over the top of his spectacles, and smiled. It was the best he could do, feeling the way he did. "It's all right," he said, feeling as foolish as he ever would. "I'm her brother— the Reverend Jeremiah McCord from Apple Valley, Alabama. We don't have the apples anymore, but the valley is beautiful as ever. Come and see us, you hear?"

Lassiter went upstairs and knocked on Cassie's door. He put his hand over his mouth when she asked who was there. He did it a second time. Cassie had a bad temper. When she opened the door, she had a piece of toasted bread in her hand and she looked ready to hit him with it.

"Wrong room," she started to say.

98

"Got any coffee?" Lassiter asked.

By then it was too late for Cassie to do anything but nod her head.

Chapter Ten

"Look Deacon, you'll get into trouble for this," Cassie said, still not recognizing him. She wasn't scared and she wasn't mad: Cassie's door had been forced too often for that. She was trying reason. Soon she would use the knee.

She gasped when he took his glasses off and threw the wool hat into a corner. It was a good act—if it was an act.

Throwing herself into his arms, she clutched him tight and said, "Oh Jesus, Lassiter," she called out, shaking as she said it. "I didn't think I was ever going to see you alive again. Oh Jesus, Lassiter, you're alive."

Lassiter held her at arms' length and smiled at her. "Us bad pennies," he said.

She tried to grab him again, teary-eyed and frantic. Lassiter held her off. "A drink, old friend," he said. He turned the key in the lock and put it in his pocket. "After that we can talk."

She came at him again. He didn't fight the hug she gave him, but he cut it short.

"I know! I know!" she said, "a drink."

There were three bottles on top of a walnut stand. Cassie picked up two, then all of them. She shook the bottles at him.

"Whisky," Lassiter said, in no hurry at all. If he had to kill Cassie, where was the hurry?

Lassiter was pretty sure now. Cassie poured too much whisky into the glass and then she dropped it. Lassiter, comfortable in a fat chair by the door, watched her bend for the spilled glass.

"I could cry," Cassie said, fetching the drink right. Her hands were shaking. "Oh God, all those men dead and the money gone."

The roses were back in Cassie's cheeks, and there was nothing Lassiter liked more than a pretty woman. Cassie poured herself a drink. After she downed it, she said, "I waited and waited at that farmhouse, Lassiter. All I could think of was you and me in San Francisco. Then I heard them coming. At first I thought it was you. When I saw it wasn't, I just got out of there, fast as I could."

Lassiter liked the chair he was in. Cassie's whiskey was good, definitely not from a bar bottle. For a girl cast-off by Texas Jack, she was doing all right for herself.

"At first I was sure it was you," Cassie said. "At the farmhouse, I mean. "You don't know what it's like, to be thinking of San Francisco,

Lassiter—Nob Hill and everything, you know—and then you have to ride off with nothing at all."

"I can imagine," Lassiter said.

Cassie said, "You got to get away. The whole country's looking for you. You must be crazy to come back here. They don't have a thing on me but they know you, Lassiter. I don't know how they know but they do." Cassie laughed. "I guess Texas Jack can't be robbed after all."

There was no reason to do anything just yet. The whiskey was good and so was the company. He waved Cassie forward with the bottle. The label on the bottle read: *de Mores Whiskey—A Quality Brand.*

Cassie was good as gold. This time her hand was steady when she poured the drink, and she said, "I got you into this, Lassiter, and I'll get you out. I got a little something saved. It's in the hotel safe downstairs. You're welcome to any or all of it."

Cassie started for the door.

"I wouldn't hear of it," Lassiter said, easy in his chair, drinking and relaxed. "You been square with me, old friend, old bedmate, and that means a lot to a man, no matter how bad things are. If I do say so, sis, they're none too good right now."

Lassiter smacked his lips over Cassie's good whisky. "That don't include the whisky," he said.

Cassie got agitated again. She'd always been like that, bold and nervous at the same time.

She found her nerve, then she lost it, then she got it back.

"You got to leave Abilene, Lassiter," she said. "That's what I'm fixing to do. I'm sick of this town."

Lassiter sat up in his chair. "Why'd you do it?" he asked. The tone was quiet, but Cassie knew Lassiter. On the other hand, he thought, maybe she didn't know him well enough.

Cassie's voice faltered. "What?" she said, going white. "What was that?"

There was no reproach, no threat in Lassiter's voice. "I think you did it, sis. I think you set me up."

She started to laugh and didn't make it. "You're crazy," she said. "My God—this is Cassie you're talking to."

Batting her eyes like the heroine in a tent show, she took a step toward him. Lassiter didn't do anything to stop her. She stopped anyway. Not being able to persuade a man with her body left Cassie at a loss.

"You pour," Lassiter suggested, holding out his glass.

Her hand shook. "Aw, you're joshing me, Lassiter. You scared me for a minute."

Cassie was trying hard to find her nerve again. A drink seemed to help. "You know you're crazy," she said. The smile she threw at him was brimming with affection.

Lassiter held up his hand. "Can it," he said. "Where's the money? I don't know what your share comes to. I don't care, long as it ain't too small. No more talk, Cassie, and no more tricks.

Be smart, sis—I don't get that money, you die here and now."

"You'd kill a woman?" she said, hate in her eyes.

"Sure thing, honey."

Cassie took the drink and walked up and down for a while. She sat down at her dressing table.

"If there's a gun in that drawer, you better leave it there," Lassiter suggested.

Cassie turned foxy. "Suppose—just suppose I have the money. Part of it anyway. Would you consider a split?"

Lassiter shook his head. "The original deal's no good now. You sort of canceled our contract when you set up that ambush. I want all of it, sis—every little dollar. And let that be a lesson to you. Now where is it?"

"You son of a bitch," she rasped, greedy enough to be brave a little longer. "Go ahead—kill me."

Lassiter set down his empty glass. It seemed like such a long time since the good times in El Paso. Cassie's eyes went wide when he showed her the Bowie knife. "Maybe I won't kill you," Lassiter said, meaning it. "Maybe I'll just mark that pretty face of yours. You figure the money is worth that?"

Cassie opened her mouth to scream but no sound came out. Before she could try it again Lassiter's hand was clamped hard across her mouth, shutting off the air. To remind her that he wasn't fooling, he put the big blade across the back of her neck. Cassie shuddered.

Lassiter said, "This is about the last chance you get. Nod your head if you're ready to talk."

Cassie nodded her head and Lassiter took his hand away. "Let me start you off," Lassiter said. He talked with the knife in his hand.

"Texas Jack set the whole thing up and you helped him."

Cassie didn't say anything. Lassiter didn't bother to get an answer. "With the kind of rep Jack's got, he had to make it look good. He had to make it look so good that nobody in his right mind would suspect he was behind it. Otherwise he'd be finished in the cattle business. He'd have company detectives on his neck for the rest of his life. He'd be finished in politics. That's why all the guns and guards."

Lassiter went on. "On the other hand, Jack meant to get that money. He knew the kind of contacts you had. So you told him the one man could do it was this fella Lassiter. He could get through the guns and guards and take the train. Another useful thing about this Lassiter—he wouldn't just take the money and run. No, sir, this fella Lassiter would stay around for the split. The rest is easy. Lassiter and his bunch ride into a trap, get themselves killed, and the money disappears. The law couldn't know how many men robbed that train, so any one of them could ride off with the money, leaving you and Jack in the clear. Nod your head, Cassie."

She did what she was told.

"Just one thing bothers me," Lassiter said. "If Jack is rich as folks say he is, why steal the

106

cattle money? Why that when he can steal legal?"

"Jack put all his cattle money into business back east," Cassie said, "and lost it. Jack is next to flat broke."

"Sorry to hear that," Lassiter said. " 'Course you're forgetting that sack of money. Where's he keeping it, sis? Lie to me and I'll know it."

"Why not?" Cassie said, the fight going out of her. "It's in the parlor car, in the safe. Jack figured nobody would think of looking there for it."

"Smart fella, Jack," Lassiter said. "Now you talk, honey, and keep it simple."

"You're going after that money again?"

"It's a thought."

Cassie started up again. "I was crazy to cross you, Lassiter," she said quickly. "Crazy—scared too. You don't know how mean Jack can be. Look, I'm telling you everything I know. If Jack knew he'd do something awful to me."

"He'll have to take his turn," Lassiter said. "Keep talking, Cassie, and maybe—just maybe —you'll come out of this in one piece."

Cassie saw hope and grabbed it. "You can still get that money. Jack's got himself a new loco-motive. He's making a big fuss about taking the dead cattle buyer back to his family in Kansas City. Says it's the least he can do to show re-spect for a friend. They're supposed to load the coffin on the the parlor car sometime today, soon as it's cleaned up and boards put over the win-dow. Traveling with the dead man, Jack gets the money out of Abilene and makes himself look good."

Cassie paused. "I'm supposed to go along for the ride."

A knock sounded on the door. With the knife at Cassie's throat, Lassiter told her to ask who it was.

"Dixon Quirly," a man's voice said through the wood.

Lassiter looked around quickly. There was a small dressing room screened by curtains. "Wait a minute, then open it," he said. "Make a move, say anything—and I'll drop you. Understand?"

Cassie nodded.

Dixon Quirly came in, sour-faced as ever. Texas Jack's top gun didn't look like a man who'd come into big money. Gun in hand, Lassiter watched from behind the curtain. Cassie asked Quirly what he wanted.

"Ain't you ready yet?" he asked. "What's the matter? You look kind of nervous to me."

"Don't you worry about me," Cassie said. "Now get the hell out of here and let me pack. I don't want you in my room."

Quirly looked mournful. "I came up the back way," he said. "I asked you what's to be nervous about? Getting rattled at a time like this could be bad. Would be a shame to have you spoil things, getting rattled."

"Get out, Quirly," Cassie ordered him.

The gunman came closer. Behind the curtain, Lassiter had to make up his mind about something. He knew Quirly was going to kill her. He could stop him and forget about the money. He thought about the old days in El Paso. They didn't mean anything, not any more.

Cassie backed away from the killer. "I said get out. Now you do it. If Jack knew . . ."

The ghost of a smile appeared on the gunman's face. "It was Jack sent me," he said. Faster than a striking rattler, a knife dropped into Quirly's hand from his sleeve. The thin blade plunged through Cassie's heart. Her eyes opened wide and stayed out. Quirly lowered her body to the floor and wiped the blade carefully on her dress. When he left, he locked the door from the outside.

Lassiter came out and looked at the dead woman for a while. He didn't feel sorry for her. He would have killed her the same way. Still it was sort of a shame. Cassie had been one hell of a woman in her day.

It was getting dark outside. He poured himself a drink and sat down to wait. There was hardly any blood from the hole in Cassie's heart. The room smelled of perfume and whisky. When it was dark enough he left the room and went down the back way.

Chapter Eleven

Pretty soon, Lassiter knew, they'd be looking for a funny looking gent that said he was Cassie McCord's brother from Apple Valley, Alabama. The hotel clerk might not remember the part about the apples. He'd remember enough to start them looking. If what Cassie said was true, there wasn't much time to take one last crack at that money before Texas Jack and his funeral train took off for Kansas City.

Lassiter went back to where his animal was tied in front of the saloon. He rode the animal into the alley between the saloon and the building next door, and quickly shucked the hat, coat, and shirt. Then he turned the animal loose. There was no use trying to take the Winchester along.

With his own hat pulled low over his eyes, he started down Texas Street in the direction of the railroad yards. There wasn't time to be cagey about it. He still had one big edge—they wouldn't figure him to be in Abilene.

There was a crowd gathered in front of the Drover's Hotel. "What time they bringing out the body?" he heard one man ask another. The other man said he didn't know—when Texas Jack was ready, he guessed. He passed the undertakers. The shades were down but there was light inside and the sound of a saw biting into wood. The undertaker was working late, trying to keep up with the brisk demand for coffins. At least one man in town was happy besides Texas Jack. Lassiter supposed Texas Jack would have a fine funeral when the time came.

Texas Street ended and beyond that was the depot, what was left of it, and beyond that the railroad yards and loading pens spread out in all directions. Lassiter went into the darkness between the depot and the last house on the street. After that he went around a loading pen full of restless cows. Five minutes later, coming in from the other side, he could see the back of Texas Jack's parlor car. There was only one guard he could see. All Lassiter could see was the man's legs walking up and down in front of the car. There could be other men inside the car, inside the caboose too. He didn't think so. Texas Jack was too smart to post a lot of guards over a train that was supposed to be empty and robbed.

Lassiter tried to remember what the inside of the parlor car looked like. It was divided into at least two compartments. There could be more. He hadn't been all that interested the night before. The guard kept walking up and down, humming as if he hated that tune. Getting rid of the guard could make some problems when Texas Jack found him missing. Lassiter was counting that Jack would be too anxious about other things to fret over it. Anyway, there was no other way to get aboard that train.

Lassiter picked his way through the darkness, thankful for the churned-up mud and cowshit the stampede had left behind. Once, his boot squelched in the mess and the guard turned his head. Lassiter stayed where he was, one foot raised. He put it down easy when the guard started humming again. Finally, he was right behind the parlor car.

There was light inside but no sound that he could hear. He put his ear to the side of the car and listened. Unless they were sitting dead still, there was nobody inside the car.

The guard, one of Quirly's riders by the looks of him, had taken off his hat and was scratching his head. He hummed some more, then he said, "Shit." The hat back in place, he started walking up and down again.

Crouched low, Lassiter went under the car. The guard heard him coming out and tried to turn around. Lassiter's gun barrel cracked him across the back of the neck, and he sagged into Lassiter's arms without a sound. Lassiter hit him again, harder this time, to make sure he really went to sleep. He propped the guard's rifle against one of the wheels of the car, to make it look as if the man had just got sick of the job and walked away. Next he dragged the unconscious guard far back behind the parlor car and dropped him behind a pile of wooden ties.

Sightseers had been coming and going all day, so the doors of the car were unlocked. Pulling his gun, Lassiter went inside. Nothing moved and nothing happened. The big Salamander safe, the biggest and toughest there was outside of a bank, sat gray and heavy against the wall. There was no point thinking about moving it. Nothing short of a block and tackle could move that safe. Even if it hadn't been bolted to the floor.

There was less time than before. Lassiter found that he'd remembered right about most of the layout. There was a kind of parlor section that took up most of the car. Past that, through an archway with looped-back brocade curtains, was Texas Jack's sleeping quarters, with a canopied double bed bolted to the floor. There was even an indoor privy. Lassiter didn't think he could hide there and he didn't want to. What he was looking for was the compartment where they stored the trunks. A show-off like Jack would be sure to have a place like that.

He found it—another folding door opening into space beside the privy. There were two trunks in there, and room for three. Lassiter climbed in there and pulled the hinged doors shut. It was about the smallest space he'd been in since that punishment box at Yuma Prison. He didn't know how long he could stand it with his legs bent under him like that.

Before, there hadn't been enough time. Now there was too much. Thinking of the girls in

Betsy Shannock's sporting house in El Paso helped a little. Betsy liked to think she ran the best cathouse in the whole Southwest, and he guessed she did. Cassie had worked for Betsy for a while in the old days, before she took up with Jimmy Voss, and he'd killed Jimmy, and. . . .

Lassiter heard them coming. There was rumbling, like a wagon. He guessed it was the hearse with the dead cattle buyer's body. Then there was a lot of talking, then feet sounding heavy on the iron steps. A voice he didn't know came in first, saying, "That's it, boys. Treat 'er gentle." That would be the undertaker directing his men.

Lassiter recognized the next voice as Dixon Quirly's. "The son of a bitch must of took off," it said.

Texas Jack Chandler told him to shut up.

After that silver dollars clinked. Texas Jack was saying to the coffin toters, "Thank you, boys, and may God bless you, one and all. You got Jack Chandler's thanks, men, and don't you forget it."

The feet went down the iron steps and Texas Jack said, "Lock the door, Quirly. Then fix me a man-sized drink."

Fixing the drink in the galley at the end of the parlor area, Dixon Quirly said, "I still don't know what happened to Stackpole. You said only one man, so I sent Stackpole. I'd of swore that boy was my best man."

A bottle rattled against a glass. "I said a man-sized drink, you sad-faced son of a bitch," Texas Jack said. "Where you from anyways, Quirly?"

Quirly's voice said something Lassiter

115

couldn't quite make out. It sounded like "Massachusetts."

"Any trouble with Cassie?" Texas Jack asked next.

"Not a bit," Quirly said.

"They're backing in the locomotive," Texas Jack said, sucking loudly on his drink.

Lassiter stiffened when he heard a woman's voice. It was dainty and Southern and it said, "Mr. Quirly's forgot me in the drink department, Mr. Chandler."

Texas Jack let out a bark of laughter, then brought it down to a chuckle. "Mr. dear departed Woodruff getting you down, honey?" he asked.

The voice was cool. "Just a little bit, Mr. Chandler. But I would like a teensy old drink."

"Well, I think that can be arranged, don't you Quirly, old shit-face?"

Lassiter figured Jack had taken on quite a load before he boarded with the dead fat man. He cursed the yard men for being so slow hooking up the locomotive. It was too quiet to start crawling out of that trunk space. There just had to be shooting and he'd just as soon the town of Abilene, all those still-irate citizens, didn't know about it. He stayed still where he was, cursing the sitffness in his legs.

"Hey, Quirly, you think one Texas drink going to last me all night?" Texas Jack complained to his black-clad man of all work.

Lassiter could hear them backing in the locomotive. A muscle in his leg started to twitch. A Comanche had put an arrow in there some years

116

back. The arrowhead had broken when it hit the bone. There were still a few pieces in there and they hurt like hell when it rained too much, or in places like the punishment hole at Yuna, or in this place.

The parlor car shook as the backed-in locomotive made contact.

"Do the honors again, will you, Quirly," the woman said.

Quirly was getting tired of playing man-servant. Lassiter grinned when he heard the killer say, "There's the bottle, miss. Get it yourself."

Texas Jack started to laugh. Remembering the dear he departed, he said, "That ain't no way, Quirly. Not for the future Mrs. Jack Chandler it ain't."

Lassiter heard Quirly getting up to get the drink.

"You really mean it, Mr. Chandler?" the woman said. She sounded more like a girl than a woman. After she squealed, she apologized. "You really mean it, Mr. Chandler? Truly mean it, I mean?"

There was the sound of couplings being dropped into place, and tested.

"We're off," Texas Jack said in great good humor. "Massa Linkin's funeral train's on its way."

"Did you really mean it?" the girl asked again. "I never dreamt . . ."

"You ain't crippled, Quirly, I don't suppose," Texas Jack called out. "In case you forget, mister, you working for a drinking man. A Texas drinking man, that is, and they don't come no drinkiner than that."

The girl thought that was about the funniest thing she'd ever heard. The trunk under him creaked as Lassiter reached back to massage his painy leg. The girl sounded like such a goddamned fool he didn't know if he wanted to kill her. He would if he had to.

A blast of steam sounded as the driving wheels began to turn. Lassiter promised himself to stay away from trains after this. He didn't know when he'd had so much to do with trains. In the end, there was nothing like a nice clean bank job. You walked in with a gun and took the money and rode out. Or you didn't. Either way it was simple. Lassiter blamed his bad humor on the pain in his leg. It was getting pretty bad and he didn't know how worse it would be by the time he crawled out of there.

The locomotive didn't pick up speed for a while—out of respect for the dead, Lassiter figured. Out past the yards he felt the throb as the engineer let loose the power. The clacking of the rail separations came faster together. Pretty soon, Lassiter thought. He didn't want to jump off too close to Abilene and he didn't want to go all the way to Kansas City or even to the Kansas line. Topeka would be just about right, maybe a little before Topeka. It was a shame he couldn't take all the money in Jack's safe. He couldn't. There was too much of it. No matter how tight you packed it, there still was too much bulk for a man to carry and get away unnoticed.

The girl giggled. "Oh, Mr. Chandler," she said. There was more giggling. Lassiter thought of the dead cattle buyer in his box. The girl said again, "You are a caution—you know that, Mr. Chandler?"

Lassiter couldn't see a thing, but he could picture the scene in his head—Texas Jack laying his big paws on the girl, who giggled every time he did it, and Dixon Quirly sour-faced as ever, trying not to look.

Texas Jack was laughing fit to die. "Well, we engaged, ain't we, honey?"

The girl said something Lassiter couldn't hear. He knew what it was.

"Aw, Quirly don't count," Texas Jack said. "That old boy's more like a monk than a man. Got iron by his side but none betwixt his legs. Ain't that right, Quirly. Well, answer the question, Quirly."

The girl said something Lassiter couldn't make out. When she was trying to wheedle a man she dropped her voice. But they all did that, this one more than most. Lassiter figured this one was new with Jack, a replacement for Cassie. She had to be just picked. Otherwise, Jack wouldn't be treating her so gentle.

Jack was out to please her all right. "Listen, my dear, me and Quirly's just fooling. Old Dix Quirly don't mind a bit, 'cause he knows I'm looking out for his welfare every minute."

The girl giggled again.

"Ain't that right, Quirly?" Texas Jack wanted to know.

"Anything you say, Jack," the gunman said.

119

Lassiter figured Quirly must be getting paid pretty good to take that kind of talk from Jack. Quirly could shoot the eyes out of Jack's head, but then the money would stop.

"Set 'em up again, Quirly, old pard," Jack was saying now. "Don't stint the booze this time. Me and the missy here got some heavy plowing to do. We ain't going to be able to stop and drink once we gets going good. Me and the missy going to plow a furrow all the way to Kansas City. 'Course the missy just going to help. I'll be the one doing most of the heavy work."

Jack roared like a fool. No matter how much noise the train made Lassiter could always hear Jack. "What do you say, sweet lips?" Jack inquired.

The train drowned out the girl's reply. Lassiter knew it would be yes. With Jack, it had to be yes.

Having Jack bed down with a woman right on the train was something he hadn't figured on. As the train picked up more and more speed, he inched open the door of the rathole where he was, and began to crawl out.

Chapter Twelve

Even with the noise of the train, it took some doing to get out of there. If Texas Jack hadn't been busting a gut with edgy laughing, it wouldn't have been possible at all without being heard. The hinged doors opened easy enough but the trunk under him squeaked. It squeaked no matter how slow and easy he moved. He stayed still for a bit. It still squeaked when he moved again. He let it squeak.

Lassiter was half in and half out, blinking his eyes to get used to the light. He could see Texas Jack but not Quirly and not the girl. What he wanted to see was Quirly. Quirly was the fast one—the one paid to be fast. After the riding Quirly had taken from Jack—and, worse, from the girl, whoever she was—the gloomy killer would be madder and faster than ever. Quirly would be the one to kill first. After that Jack.

Lassiter dragged his cramped legs down off the trunk. He was in the sleeping compartment with the big, bolted-down bed. The damn thing even had a canopy on it. He knew he hadn't moved a minute too soon, because now Jack was suggesting that they take a roll in the hay. "Nothing like it to while away a long train trip," he was saying.

Lassiter couldn't see the girl simpering, but he knew that's what she was doing.

"I told you pay no heed to Quirly," Jack said. Lassiter was close enough to the archway to see most of what was going on in the next room. Quirly was sitting by the boarded-up window, his thumbs hooked inside his belt, a look of total gloom on his lean face. They had taken out the dining table to make room for the coffin. The coffin stood on two trestles. Jack sat in a red plush armchair, with his mud-spattered white boots resting on top of the coffin. The girl, young and pretty in a washy way, was in another chair on the other side of the coffin.

"Maybe it ain't Quirly's bothering you," Texas Jack said. The idea made him bellow with laughter. He was having such a good time he drummed his boot heels on the lid of the coffin, making a hollow sound that did sound like a drum. "Could it be this old fella inside here is making you shy?"

The girl tittered. To help along the fun, Jack reached across the coffin and pinched her. Lassiter edged closer. He could have dropped Quirly from where he was, but that might give Jack time to go for his gun. He knew he could drop Jack too, except that wasn't the idea behind this train ride. With Jack dead or badly wounded the safe would just sit there.

"Look, honey," Jack said. "Mr. Woodruff ain't a-going to mind. Now you be a good girl and come to bed with Daddy Jack."

Lassiter didn't give her time to answer. Quirly jerked in his chair when Lassiter stepped through the archway. But he didn't go for his gun. "Stay still," Lassiter said easily, keeping the gun on Quirly. "Stay comfortable, Jack. Keep the boots right where they are."

He had expected the girl to scream. She didn't. Jack's hands lay flat on the arms of the chair, the matched Colts hidden by his coat. Jack's eyes bulged a bit and his red face grew dark. In a moment he forced himself to show his buckteeth in a dangerous grin.

"You'd be Lassiter," he said.

Lassiter spoke to the girl without looking at her. "You, miss, you get up nice and easy. Then you slide around that coffin and take Jack's guns. Don't get in front of him unless you want a bullet in the back. After that you take Quirly's gun. Then you toss the guns back in the galley and sit down where you were. Understand?"

"Yes sir," the girl said.

The train was taking a long curve. Lassiter braced himself, keeping the gun steady on Quirly's chest. Texas Jack's famous smile slipped as the girl reached from behind the chair and eased one gun out of its holster, then the other.

Texas Jack put his smile back in place. "Cassie said you was good. Looks like the old gal knew what she was talking about. Now look here, Lassiter, you ain't really going to take all that money? Why don't you be a nice fella and let's us talk a deal?"

"Be careful with Mr. Quirly," Lassiter warned the girl. "He might want to use you as a shield. That's the way, miss. Reach over now and take his gun."

The guns bumped on the metal floor of the galley and the girl looked at Lassiter. "Not yet," he said. "We got to de-fang this snake." He motioned Quirly to his feet with the barrel of the gun. Quirly shook the thin-bladed knife from his sleeve. The girl picked it up and tossed it after the guns. A right smart girl, Lassiter decided, in spite of the apple-pan-dowdy.

"Start on the safe," he ordered Texas Jack. "You want us to talk a deal. My deal is—open that safe and I'll let you live."

Texas Jack didn't scare easily. "Kill me and you don't make a dollar," he said. "That ain't no deal you just offered. Without that money I'm dead anyway. You started out to get forty-five thousand. All right. Take it and no more arguments."

Lassiter was sick of Texas Jack, sick of the whole business. "I'm tired," he said. "I come a thousand miles to do a job. Since that time I've been set up, lied to, shot at, and ambushed. I'm so tired I'd just as soon shoot you and forget about the money. Don't expect Mr. Quirly here to do anything. Now open that safe. You got one minute to do it."

Lassiter was as tired as he sounded. That

124

made him more dangerous than ever. Texas Jack must have known it. There was nothing to smile about now. Lassiter watched him carefully as he bent down in front of the safe and began to spin the tumblers. When the last one clicked into place, he reached for the handle, to pull the door open.

"Hold it," Lassiter said. "You did fine, Jack. Go back and sit in your chair. We'll let the lady do the honors. That's right, miss. You'll see a big canvas sack full of money. Just drag it out of there, then go back and sit down. If you happen to see a gun in that safe, don't even think aboout it."

The girl nodded.

The door swung open and Texas Jack tensed up. Lassiter relaxed him with a look. The money sack was so heavy the girl had trouble getting it out. Lassiter thought it was a shame he couldn't take all of it. He forced himself to see the practical side of it. It would be different if he had a horse ready and waiting. He grinned inside. Nothing slowed down a man on the run like a big sack of money, especially when it was white canvas lettered with the cattle company name.

"That's the girl," he said when she finally got it out of the safe. "Before you sit down, you better open that sack. It could be a sack of chopped-up newspapers."

He was being robbed, but Texas Jack saw the humor in that. "I wish I'd thought to do that," he said.

Lassiter said, "A fella can't think of everything." To the girl he said, "Not on the floor. Use the coffin."

The girl opened the drawstring and began to stack the bundles of money on the polished wood. Quirly was more interested in Lassiter than the money. Texas Jack licked his lips, like a miser in a touring play, as the stack of money grew higher.

"My God," the girl said, standing back at last. Her green eyes glittered with excitement. The money lay on top of the coffin, crisp and clean and new. Lassiter knew what the girl was thinking about.

He grinned at her. "Help yourself," he said.

Texas Jack roared, "You just wait a god-damned minute, cowboy."

Lassiter pointed him back in his chair. Quirly didn't move. The girl laughed nervously, looking quickly at Texas Jack, then back at the money. "My God," she said again, greedy and scared and confused.

"Go ahead," Lassiter told her. "This is the best chance you'll ever get."

Veins were standing out on the side of Texas Jack's thick neck. It was a pleasure to make Jack suffer, Lassiter thought. Jack looked from Lassiter's gun to the girl's face. It wasn't hot in the car, but beads of sweat glistened on her forehead. She reached out and touched the stack of bills.

"You mean it?" she asked Lassiter.

"I'll kill you, bitch," Texas Jack roared. "I swear by the Texas Christ I'll kill you."

Lassiter was having a fine time. Edging to-

126

ward the money, he began to stuff his pockets with bills. The money was in tens, twenties, fifties, hundreds. He helped himself from all the paper-wrapped bundles. It was no good just taking hundreds. He would need some small stuff too.

"Jesus, mister, you ain't just fooling me?" the girl said. She looked ready to cry. She knew Texas Jack meant it when he said he'd kill her.

Lassiter shook his head. "It'll just be going to waste," he said. "I figure old Jack won't mind. They say he's got a heart as big as the State of Texas."

He leaned against the side of the swaying car, ready but relaxed, pockets stuffed with money. They'd come a piece from Abilene. The run to Topeka wasn't that far, and he'd have to start making plans soon. The first order of business was to buy or steal a horse. After that he'd turn the animal south and head for El Paso.

Making her decision, the girl began to stuff her bag with money. Maybe watching him had taught her something, because she didn't go only for the big bills. Texas Jack watched her like a maddened grizzly. Every banknote taken from the pile was like a branding iron put to his fat rump. Even with Lassiter's gun staring him in the eye, he couldn't keep quiet. "This Lassiter's making a fool of you," he growled. "Where the hell you think you going to run with all that money?"

"Go to hell," she said. "I'll run and maybe they'll catch me and maybe they won't. For once in my goddamned life I'm going to have myself a time. I won't have to put up with a pig like you so's I can eat good food and sleep in a clean bed."

The girl turned to Lassiter. "Take me with you, mister."

"Not a chance, honey," Lassiter said. "You get to jump off when I do, but that's as far as it goes. After that you're on your own."

Texas Jack laughed and pounded the arms of the chair with the flat of his hands. Every time he looked at the girl he started laughing again. "I told you, Missy Linda," he howled. "All that money ain't going do you a bit of good. 'Cause they don't allow folks to spend money in the penitentiary."

"Dry up," Lassiter said. The girl was none of his business. He sure as hell wouldn't kick her out of bed. At the moment he had no use for her. He thought about Quirly and Texas Jack. He'd be doing the country a favor if he killed both of them. If ever two men needed killing—he was looking at them right now. But doing favors for the community wasn't and never had been his line of work. The country was full of men like Quirly and Texas Jack. It was no skin off his rump if they went on living.

"Fetch me a drink," he told the girl.

There was a wooden clock on the wall over the safe. Topeka would be about twenty miles up ahead, he figured. There was no reason for Jack's train to stop there. All he had to do was put Quirly and Jack to sleep, then swing down as the engineer slowed down coming into town. He meant to put Quirly and Jack into a real

128

deep sleep. If they had thin skulls, they might never wake up. And that, he thought, would be a sinful shame. The nice part was that Jack couldn't run to the law and complain about being robbed.

"Thanks," Lassiter said. Jack's bourbon was good, strong and easy to get down. The drink he liked best was tequila, a habit he'd picked up in Mexico, but there was nothing wrong with good bourbon.

Texas Jack had been thinking about something. After he chewed it over good, he said to Lassiter, "How much you think you got in your pockets?"

Holding the gun in his right hand, the glass in his left, Lassiter said, "Enough to last me."

"Come to work for me," Jack said, "and you'll see a lot more than that. I got big plans, Lassiter. Bigger'n you can imagine."

"I hear you're flat broke," Lassiter said.

Texas Jack laughed. "Bullshit! A man like me is never broke. Before I'm through I'm going to be the biggest man in this country. But I can't do it without a good man to side me. Quirly ain't no good except for killing."

"He's good at killing women."

Jack was talking business now. "Killing's fine when it has to be done. But a man needs to know more than that. You throw in with me, Lassiter, and I'll fix you up real good. You don't want to be on the prod all your life. Why, man, I'll even wangle you a full pardon. No more running from the law, sleeping in cold camps, chew-

129

ing on rotten jerky. With me you can step out and live like a man."

Lassiter said, "What you want is a Quirly with brains. I think you better stick with the original Quirly."

Jack wasn't ready to give up yet. Without looking at the gunman, he said, "Forget Quirly. If Quirly bothers you we'll get rid of him. Who in hell needs Quirly?"

"Hear that Quirly?" Lassiter called out. "How's that for a letter of recommendation for your next boss?"

Quirly didn't think it was funny.

Lassiter looked at the clock. It was time. Already the train was beginning to lose speed. Up front the engineer let loose a blast so Topeka would know they were coming. It was time for Quirly and Texas Jack to take a long nap.

"Just turn around, gents," he ordered them. "This ain't going to hurt a bit."

Jack stood up first. It took Quirly a little longer. Lassiter stepped toward them.

Chapter Thirteen

Jack was closer than Quirly. Lassiter raised the gun to hit him first. Jack jerked his head to one side as Quirly spun around with a derringer in his hand. The barrel of Lassiter's gun crashed against Jack's shoulder. The big man roared with pain. Quirly got off one shot before Lassiter could swing his gun around. The bullet passed under Lassiter's arm without hitting him. Lassiter put two bullets through the killer's chest before he could fire again. The two forty-fives sent the skinny gunman crashing back into the galley. With the train whistle blasting when the guns went off, there was no noise—just deadly puffs of smoke.

Texas Jack's huge fist hit Lassiter before he could turn the gun. Lassiter was big, but Jack was more like a bar than a man. The next punch caught Lassiter straight in the mouth, jarring his teeth, snapping his head back. Roaring like a savage with a skin full of whisky, Jack grabbed Lassiter's gunhand in both of his big paws and started to squeeze. Lassiter's free hand pounded away, first at Jack's face, then at his belly. It was like hitting a tree. Jack didn't even grunt.

They staggered back and knocked the coffin off the trestles. Jack bent suddenly and sank his strong yellow teeth into Lassiter's arm. The gun dropped from his hand and bounced across the rocking car. Lassiter hit Jack again in the face. It didn't do any good. Jack let loose suddenly and hit Lassiter with a right and a left. Lassiter shook the fog out of his head and made a dive for the gun. A kick in the back of the knee sent him flying across the car. Lassiter caught a glimpse of the girl struggling to get out of the way.

The gun was under Lassiter now. He rolled over as Jack's boot stomped at his face. Lassiter had the gun in his hand when another kick sent it flying again. Lassiter was on his knees trying to get up. Jack aimed a kick at his gut and missed. Lassiter grabbed Jack's heel and twisted hard. There was a crash as the big man's body hit the floor of the car. Lassiter made another try for the gun. Then Jack's bulk dropped on him like a dead horse and the big man's huge hands closed about his neck. Lassiter struggled and kicked, but couldn't break the hold. He tried to brace the muscles of his neck against the fierce strength of Jack's hands. Still choking, Jack dragged his head back, then slammed it against the floor. The blood pounded in his head as it hit the floor again.

"How'd you like that, cowboy?" Jack roared. Lassiter groaned and went limp. The hold relaxed for a moment. Putting all his strength into it, Lassiter rolled the big man off his back. Before he could break loose, Jack grabbed him again. Jack gripped his neck with one hand and clawed for his eyes with the other, but his hands were slick with sweat, and he didn't make it. Lassiter hit Jack under the nose with the heel of his hand. The big man roared with pain for the first time, and the blood started to spatter.

Clawing and punching, they staggered to their feet, then went down again, knocking the girl against the wall. Jack closed in fast. Lassiter ducked under the outstretched arms. Coming up under them, he butted Jack in the face with the top of his head. Jack's front teeth splintered and broke. Lassiter thought his skull would explode with pain. Spitting out broken teeth, Jack hit him again. Jack could have picked up the gun when Lassiter fell. Instead, he kicked it out of the way. "I'm going to kick the guts out of you, cowboy," he roared.

Lassiter dodged a kick in the belly. Jack slipped in his own blood and fell flat on his back, covering the gun with his huge bulk. Lassiter stepped in fast and kicked him in the side of the head. Jack rolled away, roaring, and Lassiter kicked him in the kidneys. Lassiter's hand was inches from the gun when Jack's kicking feet caught him in the chest and sent him staggering.

The stack of money had come loose. It was

under their feet as they kicked and punched their way back and forth the moving car. Lassiter could feel the train picking up speed again. That meant they had gone through Topeka and were heading for the Kansas line. Lassiter stood back and hit Jack again. It wasn't the best punch he'd ever thrown, but it would have flattened a smaller man. It would have broken another man's jaw. The big man, bleeding from mouth and nose, just shook his head and kept coming.

Jack wasn't much short of three hundred pounds. Some of it was fat. Most of it was solid muscle packed on a heavy-boned frame. Lassiter took a punch on the side of the neck. He tried to shake his head. It was hard to shake his head. Jack closed in throwing roundhouse swings. Lassiter dodged away. The blood-smeared money was slick as ice under his feet. Putting himself out of the way of another swing, he felt his boots starting to slide. His arms went wild trying to get his balance. Lassiter was wide open. Jack hit him hard in the belly and the wind went out of him like a blown-up pig bladder slashed with a knife. It went out and didn't want to come back in. The fog that clouded his brain closed in again and coming thickly through it he heard a wheezing noise. The fog in his head made it hard to think. Then he knew what it was—his lungs trying desperately to suck in air.

"Don't die on me yet, cowboy," Jack roared, rocking Lassiter's head with what passed for him like a light punch. Lassiter knew Jack was making a big play out of it for the girl's benefit.

Jack wasn't that great with a gun, but he was the best dirty fighter in Texas. Thoughts like that rolled around in Lassiter's head. He edged back, trying to stay out of Jack's way.

The money rustled under their moving feet. The moving feet were slow and heavy. Lassiter knew he was taking a beating. He took two more punches without going down. Jack tried to rush him. Lassiter didn't know how he managed to side-step. He didn't get out of the way, not altogether. Jack's meaty shoulder struck him a glancing blow and he crashed back against the wall. He tried to bounce off the wall like a wrestler off the ropes. It wasn't much of a try, but his rawboned frame hit Jack pretty hard. Jack didn't try to dodge or roll. He stood there and took it. It didn't even shake him.

Jack hit Lassiter with a flat-footed punch. The thick-muscled arm jerked back, then came forward like a steam-driven piston. It was aimed at Lassiter's face and it took him squarely in the center of the chest. As a boy, Lassiter had been kicked by a mean-tempered jackass. The blow in the chest felt something like that. But the jackass had kicked him only once. Jack hit him again, right over the heart. It didn't hurt more than any of the other punches. By now his body felt like one big bruise. No special hurt any place.

Now there was light in his head instead of fog. A white glare tinged with red. Jack closed in. Lassiter could feel his foul breath gusting into his face. His eyes were open but he couldn't see. Now the glare of light was nearly all red. As the light began to fade he heard a cracking noise. Then he didn't hear anything else for a while.

When he opened his eyes again the girl was bending over him. The whisky she was pouring into his mouth stung his torn lips. "I thought you were dead," she said.

Too much whisky went down too fast. Lassiter coughed and took the bottle in his own hand. The hand holding the bottle shook violently. It stopped shaking after two more drinks.

"Lay still," the girl said when he tried to get up. Lassiter did what he was told. It seemed like a good idea.

"Jack?" he said. His head felt as if it had been used for target practice. It hurt to talk, even to think.

The girl's face twisted. "I killed him," she said. "Shot him in the back with your gun. What else could I do?" She started to shake. "What the hell else could I do?"

The train was still moving, so they couldn't have heard anything up front. There was pain when Lassiter twisted his head to look at the clock. Goddamn it, he'd been out for most of an hour. The pain when he tried to get up was worse, and the girl had to help him. It had been a long time since he'd taken such a beating, if ever.

He heaved himself into the armchair and the girl handed him the bottle. Texas Jack lay face down on the floor, a gaping hole in his back. The blood looked black on the gray broadcloth. There was blood everywhere, on Jack's white Stetson, on his white boots. Lassiter tilted the bottle and drank till most of the pain went away. He didn't offer any objection when the girl got a pan of water and a clean dish towel from the galley and sponged the blood off his face. After he was finished, the girl took the bottle and drank from it.

Lassiter stood up by himself. It wasn't easy to do it without help, but he made it. At least he could do that much. How much else he could do was something to be discovered later.

Lassiter looked at her. "What do they call you?" he asked.

"Linda," she said. "And you're Lassiter. All right, Lassiter, what happens next?"

He knew he'd been wrong about this one when he figured her for a fool. He noticed, too, that the Dixie accent had been lost in the mix-up. The accent and the goddamned giggle had been part of her act for Texas. Lassiter was never hurt badly enough not to appreciate a good-looking woman.

"What're you grinning about?" she asked him.

It was a good question, he had to admit. His mouth hurt like hell when he grinned. He tilted the bottle again, letting Texas Jack's good bourbon put some fire back in his veins.

"I don't know why I'm grinning," he said. "I had figured on jumping off this train a ways back. That was when I was feeling livelier than I do now. The way I feel now, jumping off trains doesn't seem like such a good idea. You understand, sis."

"Sis!" the girl said. "I'm not your sis. Also, I

think you're most ways drunk and a little crazy. I asked you what you want to do?"

Lassiter thought about it. They were so close to Kansas City now they might as well go all the way. Anyway, he had never been to Kansas City. He'd been in Joplin and Jefferson City but not Kansas City. This was as good a time as there'd ever be. They could lay up in some fancy hotel and have themselves a time on Texas Jack's money. He'd worked had enough to get it.

The girl called Linda—he didn't know her last name and didn't want to know—said that she'd never been to Kansas City either.

"What about it?" he asked her.

"Sure," she said.

Lassiter knew he was drunk when he heard himself telling the girl it was time to go to bed. There was about an hour to go, and the bed was big and soft, and he was body sore and head weary.

"Never you mind about those dead men," he told her. "You'll get used to it after a while."

The girl laughed, a little drunk herself now. "Where you think I been, mister?" she said. "I grew up around dead men. 'Course this was the first one I killed myself."

Lassiter squinted at her. No, sir, he'd been dead wrong about this one. Jack wouldn't be the last man she killed. He liked her.

The train roared on through the night, slowing down through small towns, moving fast again when it passed through. An hour was plenty for what they had to do. Maybe Texas Jack was the first man she'd killed. He sure as hell wasn't the first one she'd climbed into bed with. It would be no lie to say she knew how to doctor a fella better than any sawbones. And she smelled a damn sight better than any doctor.

The train rocked along and Lassiter had to fight the urge to sleep. Time for that—and more doctoring—when they got to Kansas City. Lassiter still hurt from toe to top, but he felt better with each passing mile of track. He hated like hell having to get out of that big bed.

While they were pulling on their clothes, the girl said, "Too bad we can't take all of it. What do you think? It seems like such a waste to just leave all that money laying there."

Lassiter knew he'd have to watch this Linda. There was a lot about her that reminded him of Cassie. The looks were different, and the voice and the color of the eyes, but the resemblance was there. Lassiter didn't mind that. Most women were greedy. It was when they let it get out of control that you had to start worrying.

Lassiter buckled on his gun and stomped on his boots.

"Well, isn't it?" she prodded. She picked up one of the blood-smeared bills and crinkled it between her fingers. She tried to stuff it into her bag. It wasn't easy with the bag so full.

"No," Lassiter said. "We leave what's left where it is. You want to walk through Kansas City toting a sack of money? Besides, the law won't find it hard to figure things out once they find Jack and his friend. That should stop them looking for me, least for a while. A while is all I need."

"Oh hell," the girl complained.

They jumped off the train as it slowed down on the outskirts of Kansas City. Nobody saw them do it. Coming out of the railroad yards on to a broad avenue with gas lights, they took a horse trolley into the city. Lassiter still didn't know how much money he had in his bulging pockets. Enough, he guessed.

The girl snuggled up to him on the trolley. Maybe she thought it was kind of romantic. Lassiter grinned at her. She was a foxy one and he'd have to watch her. He decided to give her the usual two weeks.

No more than that.

Book Two

JACK SLADE

GUERILLA
and
THE MAN FROM LORDSBURG

Chapter One

GUERILLA

Lassiter was still trying to get his eyes used to the morning sunlight when the two guards brought him up from the solitary cells to the Warden's office. After ten days of lying chained on a wet greasy floor, with no light and only the stinking waste bucket for company, he shook with old fever and smelled like a goat.

He wore leg irons and his handcuffed wrists were fastened to a wide leather belt that encircled his waist. All he could say for ten days in the New Orleans Parish Prison was they hadn't beaten him. Not yet anyway; maybe that came next.

The guards shoved him into the office, then went outside, to wait for the Warden's call. Lassiter looked around, and after ten days of cold slime and total darkness, it was hard to believe that the world could be clean and comfortable.

Though it was late spring, a wood fire crackled in an iron grate, and a thick red-brown Turkish carpet covered every square inch of the floor. Pictures of dead or retired Wardens looked down from the walls, and there were two flags: Old Glory and the Louisiana State flag. Bright, hard sunlight slanted into the office; it seemed to sharpen the clean smell of wax polish, wood smoke, and burning tobacco.

"Stand there," the warden ordered, pointing with a cigar. Long, stiff-backed, dressed in black, the warden himself looked like a cigar. "You, prisoner, stand there, stay standing there. If you so much as . . ."

The warden was a thin-lipped old soldier, the kind that favors self-discipline and cold baths, and he glared at Lassiter, as if the caked slime on his canvas prison suit, the stink he gave off, were of his own choosing. "Do I make myself clear?" he asked.

"Yes, sir," Lassiter answered promptly, in no hurry to bring on a beating.

There were two other men in the room, standing back from the warden's desk, and it was hard to see them because of the sun. Then one of them spoke, and at first Lassiter couldn't fit a face to the voice, because it had been such a long time. But it came to him—Frank Bender.

"You don't look so good, Lassiter," the Pinkerton agent said, pushing his heavy frame away from the wall. Always a massive chunk of a man, Bender had added fat to the bone and muscle, but he was big enough to carry it. Bender looked like he had come up in the world; at least in the Pinkerton Detective Agency. Lassiter thought he looked comfortable in the good gray suit, with the heavy gold watch chain looped across his belly, and the cigar in the corner of his mouth had cost more than a nickel.

Lassiter had nothing to say to the first question,

8

so Bender tried another. "Haven't been eating regular, could that be it?" The Pinkerton detective grinned at his little joke, but the warden and the other man kept their faces stiff. Lassiter had never seen the third man before. Not much past thirty he was trying hard to look older; the wispy yellow mustache and soft face didn't go with the elderly black suit and solemn manner. To Lassiter, he looked like a self-important fool with good connections.

"Do we have to?" His voice was clipped and reedy; the question was for Bender.

"You'll have your chance, Mr. Fernald." Bender hadn't stopped staring at Lassiter. "You just let me and Lassiter have our little talk. Lassiter knows how I work. He ought to—he's given me and Pinkerton a lot of trouble. Right or wrong, Lassiter?"

"Right, Frank," Lassiter agreed. "Don't suppose you got anything to eat?"

Bender thought that was rich. "I just might, pilgrim. What'll it be? Steak and eggs, hot biscuits, coffee, apple pie? That all right with you?"

Lassiter's empty belly rumbled at the thought of food. At the same time, after ten days of bread and water, it sort of gave him a sick feeling. Bender was a mean bastard to torment a hungry man that way. Still and all, he couldn't blame the big man-catcher. Like Bender said, he had given the Pinkertons some anxious moments in his time.

"Don't fry the meat too hard," he said, and just after he said it the weakness went from his head to his legs, and if he hadn't jerked back his head the floor would have hit him in the face. Chained and tremble-gutted, he didn't try to do anything but lie there.

The warden's carpet had been cleaned recently: the smell of naphtha burned in his nose. Bright lights bobbed behind his eyes and his belly heaved, but nothing came up but air. Then, feeling the trickle of sick cold sweat, he felt himself being picked up and slammed into a chair.

He heard Bender telling Mr. Fernald to save the water he was bringing to the rescue. It was funny but his face muscles didn't want to grin. Bender said: "Water'll kill this fella. Fetch some whisky."

The brimming glass of whiskey put to Lassiter's mouth made him gag, and he gagged again as it went down his throat. It was good whisky but burned hot in his empty, shrunken stomach.

"Another one," Bender said. "That one just got his attention."

Lassiter heard Mr. Fernald complaining about giving spirits to dangerous criminals. The warden was in his own office, but he had nothing to say. "Drink up, that's the spirit," Bender said, putting the second glass to Lassiter's mouth.

With the second drink in his belly, Lassiter felt new strength creep out slowly to his fingers and toes. When he blinked he could see all right; his head felt light but clear.

Mr. Fernald picked up his gloves, hat, cane, from the warden's desk. Looking at Lassiter seemed to hurt his eyes, so he didn't look. "You understand the Governor's position in this matter," he said to Bender. "An extraordinary proceeding, if I may say so."

"It won't be forgotten at election time," Bender said.

The Governor's go-between put on his hat, tapped

it, adjusted it. He looked at the warden. "You'll join me for dinner?"

"Delighted, Mr. Fernald," the warden said.

They went out leaving Lassiter and Bender together in the quiet room. On the wall the big wooden clock wasn't loud but its ticking could be heard when the talking stopped. Lassiter, feeling better, wondered how far he'd get if he jumped Bender.

"Don't try it, friend," Bender said, pushing back his sack coat to show the chunky hammerless .45 Colt in a low-slung shoulder holster. "Wouldn't be smart."

Lassiter knew it wouldn't. "That's my thought."

Bender was a man of suddenly shifting moods, and now he grabbed the cigar from his mouth so fast it broke between his thick fingers. He cursed and threw it on the carpet and stomped on it. He changed his mind and picked up the mashed tobacco, and tossed it into the fireplace. A gray stain remained after he finished rubbing the ash into the carpet with the toe of his boot. "Bullcrap," he said, reaching for another cigar. "You notice they didn't invite me along? They could have but they didn't." Bender bit off the end of the cigar, went to the fireplace to spit. "They could have."

Lassiter was tired. "Guess so, Bender."

That wasn't enough to cool down the Pinkerton man's flare-up. "Sure they knew I had work to do. Talking to you, you crooked son of a bitch. That doesn't mean they couldn't ask."

Lassiter said sure.

Bender broke the second cigar and threw it in the fire. Maybe wrecking the Warden's cigars like that

11

put him in a better humor. "Ah, what am I talking to you for."

"Why are you?" Lassiter wanted to know.

"In a minute, thief." Bender filled a glass of whisky for Lassiter, then fixed his own drink. They put the drinks away and suddenly Bender was all business.

Bender said: "You been ten days in the hole. How'd you like to stay there for good. I can fix that, if you like?"

"You talk, I'll listen."

"That's right, friend. I'm putting the cart before the horse, so you'll understand how bad it can get. Not that you're a horse—you're a mule."

Lassiter said nothing.

"I can get you twenty years," Bender said. "For what? I don't know for what. Lots of things. Plenty of old stuff. Maybe the Shawnessy robbery—that's new stuff."

Lassiter had no answer for that, but Bender told him to button up. "We—Pinkerton—don't have to prove anything to a jury. Not to a jury, to nobody."

Bender spread his hands like a San Francisco rug dealer. "You know that. Hardly a jury in the country wouldn't be glad to oblige Martin Luther Maddox. You know who he is?"

Bender went on without waiting for an answer. "Martin Luther Maddox is just one of the biggest railroad men in the country, that's all—and your partner in the Shawnessy robbery murdered his son."

Bender waited to see what effect his words had, but Lassiter had nothing to say about the Shawnessy robbery and the man who doublecrossed him.

12

Not yet.

"Maybe you don't know that part of it," Bender said. He grinned. "After your partner, the Spanish fella, took your share of the robbery and set the Natchez police to hunt you down, he took a riverboat south to New Orleans. Only he didn't get that far, not by boat. Downriver from Natchez he got into a poker game. Maddox Junior was in the game and caught him cheating. Your friend shot him dead, then jumped overboard with a satchel in his hand. A real strong swimmer, they tell me."

"Stop beating the bushes," Lassiter said. "What's the deal?"

"Not so fast, thief. First I better explain what'll happen if you say no. I'll get you life, so help me. You heard of Angola Prison, I'd say. The worst prison in the State of Louisiana, maybe in the country."

"Not worse than Yuma."

"As bad, in a different way. Well, friend, that's the dark side of my story. Here's the bright side: Martin Luther Maddox wants the man that murdered his son. Tried and hung preferably, but he'll settle for just plain killing the son of a bitch. You want the job?"

"Sure," Lassiter said. "Now let me ask one. With all Maddox's money, all you smart Pinkerton fellas, how come you can't catch one man?"

"Because you're the only one knows what he really looks like. You spent time with him. You had to. How much time?"

Lassiter grinned at the Pinkerton agent. "You ask questions, but you don't answer any. What's the deal?"

"You get to walk out of here. We could send a

dozen agents after this fella, but we're looking for a man with real interest in his work. That's you, cowboy. How many times you been doublecrossed in your life? This makes it the third time. They tell me the first two fellas are dead."

"So they tell me, Bender."

"Do the same for this gent and you can forget about the Shawnessy job. Never was any hard evidence against you, just this doublecrosser's say-so. That old business between you and me is long in the past. Pinkerton doesn't want you except for this job of work. Tell you the truth, it's sort of between you and me and Mr. Maddox. But you got to give your word."

"That's all it takes?"

This old man-catcher was a strange cuss all right. Bender looked surprised at Lassiter's question. "You give it, I'll take it, except . . ."

"Except what?"

Bender got mad again. "Don't you get smart with me, thief. This isn't me talking, it's Mr. Maddox. He's the one letting you go, so you'd better listen to him. Maybe you think you can give your word, then go about your business, forget about his dead son. Not so, Mr. Maddox says. You run out and he'll find you. No place in North or South America that his money—his hired gunmen—won't catch up with you."

To Lassiter that sounded reasonable enough; the sort of thing he would do himself. It was what he was planning to do himself, just before he'd landed here in the Parish Prison. "How'd you tie me into this?" he asked Bender.

Now that Lassiter was on his side, Bender stopped

14

being so careful when he moved around. He got the bottle and poured two drinks. He fished a big turnip of a watch from his vest pocket and snapped the cover open with his thumb-nail. He put the watch away.

"We're getting better all the time. We got it so organized we get copies of just about everything. Wanted posters, even if the man isn't wanted by us. Robberies, jailbreaks, so on." Bender grinned. "Pretty soon fellas like you will be a thing of the past."

"Doesn't seem sporting somehow," Lassiter said. Now he was ready to eat, but he wanted his next meal to be outside the stinking prison.

"I got word the Natchez authorities were interested in a gent named Lassiter." Bender looked pleased with himself. "Only one Lassiter I knew, so I got interested myself. Natchez wanted you for blowing the Shawnessy Company safe. That partner of yours did a good job on you. Modern, up-to-date. Used the telephone. Gave your name, description, what you liked for breakfast. You got away but Natchez tied you in with a young Spanish or Mexican fella. A couple of days later, when I got word about young Maddox, I began to add it up. Well, sir, I figured since this fella was heading for New Orleans when he killed Maddox . . . I figured you'd follow him there. That's how you got caught."

"But you missed him."

"Nearly caught him," Bender said. "We had our local agents plus the whole New Orleans police department looking for him. You know how many young greasers there are in this city? Too many. Finally we heard that some young Spanish looking

15

fella tried to swindle J.T. Andrus out of a shipment of Winchesters. The description we got from the riverboat was sketchy, but it sounded good enough. That kid ought to be laying in chains at the bottom of the river by now. That's J.T.'s way with crooks."

"But he got away." Lassiter didn't know why he was grinning. So far the son of a bitch had outfoxed everybody, especially him.

Bender said:

"He shot Andrus and got away south on a boat for Vera Cruz. Without the guns—the folks down in Quintana Roo are going to be mighty disappointed when he shows up without the guns. You know where Roo is?"

Lassiter did, more or less. "How do you figure he's gone there?"

"Part figuring, some guessing," Bender said. "Right now that's the only part of Mexico having serious trouble. I figure your boy's some kind of patriot. Maybe Roo's not even part of Mexico. The Mexicans lay claim to it, so does Guatemala. A rebel named Sandoval says it belongs to the people, whoever they may be. This Sandoval wants to start a whole new republic. The United Lumber Company, not to mention the United Rubber Company, don't bother Sandoval one little bit."

"Naturally they're planning to do something about it?" Lassiter knew how the big companies worked. When bribery didn't work, they hired guns. He gave a tight grin. What the hell was he bellyaching about? He had earned good money selling his gun to big companies. But that didn't mean he had to like the bastards.

"Not troops, mind you." Bender was grinning for

16

his own reasons. "We don't do that kind of thing nowadays. At least not in Mexico. So it's no troops, nothing official. What we have in mind"—Bender stressed the *we* to show how cozy he was with the business pirates—"is more like a fact-finding expedition. Sure they'll be armed—all those bandits and snakes . . ."

Bender paused. "You'll be going along."

Lassiter could see that Bender was pleased with his explanation of how the lumber and rubber companies planned to invade a foreign country. Later he'd probably repeat the same story many times.

"How many fact-finders?" Lassiter asked.

"Not more than a hundred to start with. All good men, all experienced. Mexico should be rooting out this Sandoval, but President Diaz has his own problems up north. Besides, Quintana Roo is a long way from Mexico City, and Diaz isn't even sure he owns the place. So he'd rather we did the job. So would we. Hell, lumber and rubber won't want to start a war—just run off this Sandoval or kill him. Business down there has been lousy since he started burning and killing."

"Sounds lively," Lassiter remarked.

"Never you mind that. You get the man that . . . you know, we don't even know the bastard's name."

"Betancourt, that's the name he gave me. It could even be real. Doesn't matter—I'll know him when I kill him." Lassiter thought back to the night three weeks before when he met Betancourt, so called, in Corley Harkins Saloon in the Irish Channel. Corley's place was the toughest saloon in the toughest section of New Orleans. Corley talked to Lassiter in private, said there was a Spanish fella who needed help to

17

blow a fat safe up in Natchez. Corley had sold him the plan, so it was a sure thing. This Betancourt, a real Spanish gentleman, according to Corley, paid five thousand for the plan, so Lassiter would be working for a flat fee.

"It could be his real name," Lassiter said. "He talked a lot. I guess he didn't see himself as a professional robber."

Bender laughed. "Professional enough, I'd say. Played a hard case like you for a fool."

That didn't bother Lassiter; in the dungeon it might, not now. "We'll see who's the professional. One of these days we will." He wasn't just talking to show Bender how hard he was. Corley Harkins said there was fifty thousand in the Shawnessy Company safe. The deal was ten thousand for him, forty for Betancourt.

"I didn't figure he'd cross me for ten thousand," he told Bender. "Not when he had forty free and clear. Maybe I got careless. We pulled the job—no trouble—and were back at the boarding house counting the money . . ."

"What did he hit you with?"

Lassiter's grin was sour. "A God damned washjug. I was supposed to be laying there when the police came running. Only I wasn't. Betancourt should have hit me harder, should have killed me. That ten thousand is going to buy him an awful lot of grief."

"That's the spirit, boy." Bender took out his watch again and looked at it.

Someone knocked on the door.

"Right on time," Bender said.

18

Chapter Two

Bender raised his voice and told the guards out-side to unlock the door, and when it was open one of the tallest men that Lassiter ever saw came in. If there had been more meat on his bones he would have gone close to the two-hundred-and-fifty mark. He was tall and wide shouldered without being heavy, and from the looks of him he was creeping up on sixty, but when he got closer Lassiter saw that he wasn't much past forty.

"Everything set?" Bender asked.

"Everything set, Mr. Bender."

The tall man looked like a sheep; even without the stuck-out ears and long nose he would have looked like a sheep. He even had sheep's eyes, yellowish, mournful. Lassiter looked at the '73 Colt in the tall man's opened holster. The holster was greased and the front sight on the long-barreled Colt had been filed off.

"Any questions?" Bender asked.

"No questions, Mr. Bender," the tall man answered. The tall man was Bender's echo, and Bender liked it. He rubbed his hands before giving Lassiter a long dust coat to cover the filthy uniform until he took a bath.

"Who's your friend?" Lassiter asked him.

Bender's barking laugh sounded like a jammed rapid-fire gun. "You won't like this, friend. On this trip you get company. Me—Hell no!" He patted his fat-padded belly. "No more rough duty for Francis K. Bender. There's your traveling companion, a good man, the best. Say howdy to John Callaway."

Lassiter said howdy.

Callaway took it as a serious question. "I'm right well, brother. And yourself?"

"Christ!" Lassiter said.

"Christ can't help you." Bender was grinning again. "Brother John goes with you—or you stay. Comes trouble you'll be glad to have him along."

"Amen," Brother John chimed in.

That seemed to settle it for Bender. He said, "You fellas go first, I'll follow along."

The guards let them out, and Lassiter followed Callaway down iron steps. At the bottom, Callaway said, "This way, brother, this door."

Out in the prison yard a thin cold spring rain splashed on grey stone. It came down mixed with city smoke and shoot, but after ten days in the hole it felt good in Lassiter's face. Up in one of the cell blocks some poor bastard was singing. Lassiter spat and after that his mouth tasted better.

They went across the exercise yard past a group of prisoners in striped suits marching in a circle in lockstep. When they got to the first gate the guard looked over their heads and got the nod from

Bender. Another guard turned a wheel that opened the inner gate.

They went through the outer gate, and Lassiter turned to look back at the squat bulk of the prison. Jesus! It was good to get away from that greasy pile of stones. Now what?

A horse cab with an elderly Negro in the box was at the curb, waiting. Callaway motioned for Lassiter to climb in first. The driver didn't have to be told where to go. "My guns?" Lassiter started to say.

"Waiting for you, brother," Callaway answered. The cab turned a corner into a wide street. Two streets from there Lassiter smelled the fishy, rotting stink of the river.

Without turning his head, Callaway said, "Bitterness and resentment ain't the way, brother. God has delivered you from the dark dungeon. But what about the dark dungeon of your soul? How long since you pondered on that question, brother?"

"Not lately, brother." Lassiter turned to Callaway and said, "If you and me have any chance of getting along, you got to stop that brother business."

The cab went down Front Street, and when they got to Jimmy Phelan's World Famous Oyster Bar Callaway told the driver to hold up. Lassiter guessed the elderly black driver didn't qualify as a brother, because all John Callaway was, "Hold up there, Uncle."

Lassiter knew Phelan's, had been there a few times. Phelan's, close to the waterfront, wasn't swank like Brennan's in the French Quarter, but maybe the food was as good, or better. It didn't have to be nearly as good; the food smells coming through the swinging doors made Lassiter weak in the legs.

23

Callaway was climbing down from the cab with a leather bag in his hand.

"You can wash first or eat first," he said. "You decide to eat first, they'll mind the stink you give off, but it don't bother me. Doesn't bother me, shouldn't bother them. I'll explain."

To hell with how he looked; Lassiter wanted to eat. He went in first followed by Callaway, and before the doors stopped swinging a big Irishman with a broad face not much different in color from his carroty hair got up from a table and got in their way.

Pushing back his gray billycock hat, the Irishman jerked a meaty thumb in some direction, maybe northwest. His brogue had an overlay of New Orleans dock talk. Maybe he had been drinking too much and needed to work off the flab. He was ready to fight. He said, "The Gospel Mission's on Girard Street, boys. Should you be Catholics, which I doubt, you'll find Father DeCourcy's soup kettle waiting for you two streets from here. Begone, lads, take yourself away from here."

"Or what?" Lassiter asked the question.

Callaway edged Lassiter to one side, and this was one time Lassiter didn't mind side-stepping a fight, though Brother John Callaway looked to be no match for the brawny mick. Phelan's was shaking with loud talk and louder music from a mechanical harp; only the drinkers and eaters at that end of the saloon knew what was going on.

The mick's name was Mick, and, like all saloon bouncers, he had his admirers. A jittery, jaunty gent in a straw boater and celluloid collar looked up from his fried shrimp and German beer. "Sic 'em, Mick," he said.

"Both of you—out!" The Irishman jerked his flat thumb; the words were final.

Callaway didn't even change his expression when the Irishman, after taking a good look at the tall .sheep-faced man, stepped back a pace and peeled back his coat to display a shoulder-holstered gun. Callaway hardly seemed to move his hand at all, but suddenly the long-barreled '73 Colt was touching the bouncer's belly.

At no loss for words, the Irishman said, "At your service, mister."

"A table for two," Callaway said with no humor at all.

"This way, sir." Bested by Callaway, the Irishman held no malice. In the French Quarter they would have called the city police, but Phelan's was Phelan's.

A waiter showed them to a quiet table; they had got past the Irishman, so it had to be all right. Lassiter sat down enjoying the sounds, the sights, the smells. For a man with such fast hands, Callaway was kind of creaky when he sat down.

"I told you I'd explain," he said, no boast in his voice. Turning to the waiter, he said, "Be not in a hurry, brother. Eternity's out there waiting on us all."

But the waiter was impatient, and so was Lassiter. He gave his order, a long one full of foods that didn't match—steak, eggs, red snapper, batter-dipped shrimps, gumbo, hot corn bread, pecan pie, coffee.

Callaway, the godly, was trying to beat back the temptations of the flesh. At last, he gave in. "May the Lord forgive me—I'll have the same."

The waiter had brought two glasses, a bottle and cigars. Lassiter hadn't decided about Callaway, but he grinned. "Amen, brother. Amen!"

"No need to mock." Callaway was pious, though not pious enough to call the waiter back and punish himself with nothing but warm buttermilk. He repeated his statement. "No need to mock. Man is frail, a constant prey to temptation. You'd do well to think on that . . ."

Lassiter had a head for names and places; you had to, in his line of work. It was like Frank Bender's voice putting a face in his mind, after all the years. A picture clicked into place in his head, just like an adjusted stereo view of the Grand Canyon, or the Garden of the Gods, in Colorado.

"You're Sheep Callaway," he said. Years back, many years back when he was pulling his first jobs, and wondering where he'd go from there, he had seen John Sheep Callaway on old wanted posters. Lord, that wasn't so long after the War, the late Sixties, the early Seventies. Lassiter, no keeper of time, couldn't be sure; the small things he recalled were linked to more or less important events. Callaway was after the War and before Custer got himself killed.

A prey to temptation, Callaway was at the bottle. "You pegged me," he said. "Famous though I was it's no cause of pride to me." That wasn't good enough, or bad enough. "Not to this sinner," he ended. Pushing his nose in the dirt called for another drink of Phelan's whisky.

"Your business, Sheep." Lassiter, waiting for his food, remembered the stories about Callaway's nick-

26

name. Back in the saloons, mostly in El Paso in the old days, the talk was that John Callaway liked sheep. That, as Lassiter recalled it now, was after they sent Callaway to Huntsville Prison to serve a life sentence for killing an express guard in a train robbery.

Callaway didn't answer until the waiter brought the food and went away. They wanted it all together, and that was all right, because it was Jimmy Phelan's.

"Dig in," Callaway said, as if the matter of sheep hadn't been mentioned. Lassiter looked at the heaping platters of food, then decided maybe he needed another drink to get his stomach prepared.

Speaking through a mouthful of fried shrimp, Callaway said casually, "As a kid I looked like a sheep—God's just punishment, I'd say—so folks called me Sheep. Wasn't true, the other stories, the dirty ones. Some fella started the name. It used to bother me—no more."

"Sure thing"—and Lassiter meant it sincerely.

Callaway said: "I don't care what you think."

What Lassiter said next was just as honest. "Me neither, Brother John. Now suppose you add a few more pieces to this puzzle."

Try as he would, Brother John was tempted by whisky. Godly man or not, he wanted to talk about himself. That wasn't what Lassiter had in mind, but he was ready to listen. You listened and learned; sometimes you did.

Just telling he was a Texas man born and bred made Callaway reach for the bottle. "May God forgive my bragging," he told Lassiter, "but I'm a Texas man born and bred and how can I help it?

27

Not a Texan but a Texican, a native born citizen of the blessed Republic of Texas, and I got citizen papers signed by General Sam Houston to prove it. You may be an American, my friend, but you're looking at a Texican. None of your Presidents never signed no citizen papers for me that I recall."

Before the waiter came with the bill, Callaway gave Lassiter fifty dollars expense money provided by Frank Bender. Lassiter thought that showed a nice sense of timing, but he told Callaway to pay his own way. "Render unto Caesar and so on, brother," Lassiter said, grinning, still stinking under the dust coat, but feeling better all round. He stood up, walked to the bar to buy a bottle, and was ready to take a bath. Callaway picked up the bag.

They walked down Front Street to Lamartine's Bath-house. Beyond that the street opened onto the docks where the air was full of salt and fresh fish, bananas and pulpy fruit from Central America. Add frying food and the beery fog from Shenstone's Brewery—and the air was thick enough to taste. To Lassiter, after ten days and nights in greasy darkness, it was like perfume from Paris.

Lassiter went wild with Bender's money and took a two dollar tub. A man could soak for as little as fifty cents, but Lassiter didn't think just a half dollar's worth of soap and water would ever get him clean.

For two dollars you got a tub in a room with a door that could be locked from the inside. They went up to the second floor. No, Callaway said, he didn't need a bath himself, but he'd sit around and wait.

They went inside and Lassiter ran the water, filling the tub with water hot enough to cook an egg. Callaway put the suitcase on a small table and unsnapped it. "All your duds washed and clean," he said, holding up things. "Your gunbelt, Colt .44, no rifle, but we got a nice new one down at the ship. Had to get you a new shirt. From the looks of the old one you gave those city police a right good fight before they took you in."

Easing himself into the tub, Lassiter knew how a boiled chicken felt. Christ, it felt good. Time enough to make suds and start scrubbing with the long-handled back brush and the Florida sponge. He already had a cigar between his teeth, so he reached over the side of the tub to get the bottle. He popped the part-pulled cork with his thumb and took a drink.

Callaway was sitting awkwardly looking at the backs of his hands. When he heard Lassiter drinking again he looked up. "Appears to me you take life too lightly," he remarked. "Now me, the first time I walked out through the gates of Huntsville Prison I got down on my knees and offered thanks to my Savior."

Thumbing the cork back into the bottle, Lassiter set it down carefully on the tiled floor. "The first time? What do you mean, the first time? How did you get out at all?"

That surprised Callaway. "I ain't out," he said. "By law I ain't supposed to never get out. Mr. Bender says some day maybe—if I keep on the right road like I been doing—but I don't set my sights too high."

Lassiter let him go on.

Callaway said, "I ain't truly out because I got to

29

go back when this job is finished. Like the other jobs Mr. Bender sent me on. Course this going to Mexico is the farthest I'm ever likely to get from that prison. Before this the longest I been from Huntsville was the time I followed that fella clear up to the Indian Territory."

Now Lassiter got it, and while it didn't spoil the taste of the whisky, the feel of the yellow soap soaking away the prison dirt, it didn't add to his enjoyment. "Why, reverend, you're nothing but a boot-licking trusty and convict man-catcher."

"Not just," Callaway said with no boasting in his flat Texas voice. "The best there is, my friend. In my forty-four years I hunted just about everything that walks. Maybe the best tracker and hunter in Texas before I turned to a life of sin and criminality. Not a man I ever went after got away from me."

Lassiter dipped the burning cigar in the bath water and threw it on the floor. "Bender tell you to say that?"

"No, sir," Callaway said mildly. "And I wasn't threatening you, if that's what you think. You asked me and I was telling you. Course I wouldn't want you to bad-mouth Mr. Bender because that man been good to me. Just remember you asked me, so I told you."

"Tell me some more."

Callaway joined his big rawboned hands and cracked his knuckles. His voice was calm, even, flatter than ever. "Might do you good to hear my story," he said. "Don't you worry, won't make it long, no longer than it takes you a-scrubbing. Sure I was a terrible wild fella when they first put me behind those high walls. All my life, a half-wild boy

30

up in the Davis Mountains, then later when I come down—just as wild. Wild and free, wasn't nobody going to keep me locked up for life."

"Yeah," Lassiter said.

"Broke out three times." Rubbing the graying stubble on his long face helped Callaway to remember when that was. "So long ago, not sure now. Anyway, broke out three times in two years. They couldn't add nothing to a life sentence, so they flogged me."

Callaway's face showed sudden surprise. "One time I did six months in solitary. By golly! Now wasn't that something?"

Lassiter got out and got a towel. He had given his word to Bender, but he was ready to kill the son of a bitch when he got back. Maybe slapping that foxy smile all over Bender's fat face would resurrect certain old problems with the Pinkertons, but he'd be damned if he'd let Bender get away with siccing a watchdog like Sheep Callaway on him.

After Callaway threw pants, undershirt, shirt across the small room, he said: "You want to know how me and Mr. Bender got to be such good friends."

Lassiter said: "Go on, tell me, or I'll wet my clean pants."

Callaway handed Lassiter his gunbelt, the .44 Colt in the holster. He gave Lassiter clean socks, then his boots.

"No need," Lassiter said. "Bender had some case that went back a ways, thought you might know something about it. Somebody you knew, something you knew. You ran wild a good many years before they caught you, reverend. You had to know things

31

Bender didn't—about jobs."

Lassiter's hat was crushed from being in the bag; Callaway worked on it carefully, plumping out the creases with his thumb. Lassiter reached over and grabbed it. "You know what you are, reverend?"

"Can't insult me, using that tone, nor any hard words in your mind. Sure my talks there at Huntsville with Mr. Bender put more than a few poor fellas in the same place, and not just there but other prisons. Mr. Bender brought me a Bible, talked long and kindly to me, said by turning those fellas in I'd be doing them a favor. Reading my Bible—Mr. Bender's Bible—told me that man was right."

Lassiter pulled on his boots, stomped hard on the bathhouse floor to make his feet comfortable. The .44 Colt was riding easy in his holster, but it wasn't the fast draw he'd seen at Phelan's that stopped him from cutting loose this trusty watchdog with a bullet. God damn Frank Bender to hell! And he God damned himself harder than that for giving his word before the deal with Bender had been spelled out to the very last word.

He was just being mean about it when he said, "They ever ask you to hang anybody at Huntsville, reverend. You being so helpful and all?"

"Only one time." Callaway might have been recalling the first time he broke a tooth. "Shafter, the hangman was kept home tending to a sick child. Wasn't nobody else, so they asked me. Didn't pay me though, they don't pay the convicts."

Lassiter took in a breath and let it out slowly. Working with this geezer was going to be one hell of an experience. "You try to be helpful all the time, don't you? Be a true blue sport and don't try to help

32

me. We got to work together, so I'm asking you that."

"The Bible says we got to help our brothers." Callaway's long sheep-face said he meant it sincerely.

Lassiter meant what he said: "That could be downright dangerous, if you press it too hard."

Callaway, holding the door open, had other ideas. "Not to a man on the right side of the Lord," he said.

Chapter Three

It was still a few hours to sunset when they walked down to the Front Street docks and went aboard the small coastal steamship *Judah P. Benjamin*. Another steamer of about the same tonnage was moored alongside. That ship's name was the *Lafayette*, and it looked to Lassiter as if the old names had been painted out and the new ones put in their place in a hurry.

Callaway had been there before, and the two men guarding the gangplank knew him, but he had to show a signed letter from somebody before the two company gunmen let Lassiter follow him on board. The *Judah P. Benjamin* had the Stars and Stripes drooping at the masthead, not a sign of any flags from the lumber and rubber interests. And once they got close to where they were going, Lassiter felt damn sure the U.S. flag would be hauled down.

"Down here," Callaway said, jerking a thumb.

Big steam launches covered with tarpaulin were lashed to the deck. Going below with Callaway leading the way, Lassiter breathed in the heavy stink of raw rubber. By the time they got below the rubber stink was thinned—or thickened—by the stink of too many men on a small boat on a hot day. Bulkheads had been cut through to the cargo holds; the doors were open and a rumble of rough voices came through. The stink of beer and whisky drifted out as though carried by the noise.

"Not in there, this way," Callaway said, nodding at a door. Another company gunman stood in front of it, a big box-shouldered German or Swede with pale eyes and paler hair. For a man going to the tropics he was dressed oddly, a new blue serge suit and a gray curve-brimmed derby. Lassiter, waiting for Callaway to show his magic letter, hoped the company thug wouldn't get too hot in that foolish get-up.

"Yah, you go in," the gunman said, pulling at his shoulder holster through his coat to make it ride better under his arm.

When the door opened Lassiter half expected to see Bender, but he wasn't there. A few years back Bender would have been there. Well, that's what happens when you come up in the world and hobnob with robber barons, Lassiter decided. The world gets safer, more comfortable, but you get to miss the excitement.

So far there was no excitement; they might have been going into a quiet, well furnished, if small, business office in a respectable commercial block. The man who opened the door was old enough to be called a man, but a lot of boy still stuck to him. His hair was light brown, parted in the middle and brushed down behind his ears. Lassiter had seen and talked to a few Englishmen in his time. The boy-man looked that way, but when Lassiter listened to his voice he knew the kid wasn't English—just trying to be. That, he knew, was the rage back East.

"Yes, my good man," he said to Callaway.

Fumbling for his letter again, Callaway didn't say anything for the moment.

Lassiter couldn't help it. "He's a good man—so he says—but I'm not."

"What? What's that you say?" The kid opened the door wider to get a better look at them. He smiled quickly, nervously. "You must be Lassiter?"

"Why must I?"

The answer was quick, like the smile, kind of sharp. The kid had a reddish mustache over strong good teeth that stuck out. Having teeth like that seemed to annoy him in an absent-minded way. Every few seconds his tongue came out and felt how they stuck out. "You don't have to be, if you don't want to."

A hoarse, wheezy old man's voice came out from behind the fancy bucktoothed kid. "What's going on there, Spencer? What's all that talk?"

Half-turning, Spencer said, "Callaway *and* Mr. Lassiter, I think."

He opened the door all the way to let them through, and Lassiter saw a hog-fat old man with a naturally red face made more red with too much rich food, even more liquor than food, with maybe weekly visits to a Turkish bath thrown in. Lassiter didn't know what the fat man was dressed like—or for. Maybe that's how the commodores of yacht clubs dressed. It sure as hell was a uniform, a snowy white uniform except where booze and grease drippings had made it dirty. There was some red and blue piping along the seams and the collar had stars and the shoulders had admiral's or general's bars.

"Ah, Callaway," the fat man said without much welcome in his voice.

Lassiter had spent much time in Mexico, mostly in the northern states, Sonora and Chihuahua, but he had never seen such a fancy uniform. Well, he was right. The fat man, waving a leg of roast duck in one hand and shaking a glass of wine in the other, was a real commodore. He said so.

"I'm Commodore Ambrose Talbot Ruffin, and don't waste my time, sir. I'm a busy man. If you're not Lassiter, get off my ship."

Callaway had his letter ready, but the fat man waved it away with a swollen, impatient hand.

"He's Lassiter," Callaway said, and begged the commodore's pardon.

The commodore was rude as well as fat. He turned his thick neck to speak to the young dude he called Spencer. "I don't know what he's doing here, I swear I don't. Why can't Martin Luther ever do things in a straight-forward manner. If someone killed my son I'd be down there gun in hand. However . . ."

That "however" told Lassiter that Commodore, for all his manner and fancy uniform, was very much beholden to Martin Luther Maddox. Maybe the Commodore put on a big front for some company, but ten to one that company was owned by the savage old railroad tycoon. So it went in the world of business, Lassiter knew. The idea, coming to him suddenly was downright foolish; still and all, he was glad he wasn't a part of it.

Callaway stood straight, respectful, like the prison

trusty he was; Lassiter saw a chair and sat in it.

The Commodore's face got redder than it had been. "No one gave you permission . . ." he began.

"Perhaps we'd better," Spencer said.

That sank in, the faint threat or reminder that Commodore Ambrose Talbot Ruffin was holding up Maddox business. "All right," he said shortly.

"What's the drill?" Lassiter looked around for whisky, but the only bottle on the fat man's desk had wine in it. Lassiter didn't like wine.

"You have nerve, sir—I like that," the commodore began.

Lassiter didn't see that it took much nerve to sit down.

The commodore said: "We're going down to Quintana Roo to teach those bandits a lesson they won't forget. Fifty men to this ship, fifty men to the other. Two landings, one on the north coast of Roo, one to the south. We on this ship will make the southern landing. That's where Sandoval has been hitting us hardest, and that's where I'll land, by God. Mr. Spencer there is my second-in-command. He'll set you straight. That'll be all."

Going out, Lassiter grinned inwardly. Sandoval the rebel would be shaking in his high-heeled Mexican boots if he could see the leaders of this expedition. Rubber and lumber were doing what the Army did all the time, which was to collect a bunch of pretty good fighting men and then put a fool in command.

Lassiter and Callaway followed Spencer up on deck. It was starting to get dark; lights showed all over what they could see of the city. The real captain of the *Judah P. Benjamin* climbed up from the engine room with the first mate behind him.

Spencer turned briskly. "Good evening, Captain Dunnock," he said. "Are we ready to cast off?"

Dunnock, a thick bodied man about sixty with a clipped mustache, was Scotch and sour and cautious about everything. "The evening is fine, Mr. Spencer. Those men of yours below are not so fine. You better get them in shape before we sail. It might not be so easy once we're at sea."

Listening to the noise below decks, Lassiter saw the Scotchman's point. Some company thug with a liking for music had pulled out a concertina and the clapping and foot pounding could be felt through the deck. It was the kind of party that could end only one way. Put fifty hard-cases together, fill them with whisky, and it had to end with knives and broken bottles, maybe with bullets.

Lassiter could see that young Spencer was looking forward to some great adventure. It showed in the flushed face, the brisk nervous walk. The commodore's fair-haired boy didn't want the Scotchman poking holes in the gallant spirited picture he was painting in his head.

"The men are simply having a good time," he told the captain in a stiff voice. "Men going off to fight must be given some leeway. I'll end the party the moment we sail. No need to worry."

Lassiter figured the Scotchman had been at sea for more than forty years, and that would take him back to the days of slave ships and the last of the pirates. "You're the one who should worry, Mr. Spencer," the captain said. "I'm too old for that."

Captain Dunnock and the first mate went to check the rigging on the steam launches that were placed where the lifeboats should have been.

"Gloomy old buzzard," Spencer said to Lassiter, who was looking at the lights of New Orleans and wondering if they still had that big wild Honduran girl at Madame Gertie's sporting house on Girard Street. That one was an oddity in the business; she loved her work and could get excited about every new customer.

"The captain's right," Lassiter said. "Those boys down below aren't regular Army, or any kind of army. You don't let them get this worked up with whisky, then walk in and say the party's over."

Being prodded twice was too much for Spencer. "We'll see about that," he snapped, making for the companionway.

Lassiter grinned at Spencer's stiffened back. "I'd like to. Mind if I come along?"

Spencer told him to suit himself. Before they got down to the big door cut through the bulkhead to the cargo holds an empty whisky bottle sailed out and broke like a bomb. Spencer moved broken glass with the toe of his boot and went inside. Lassiter grinned again. He knew the young dude wasn't feeling as cool as he looked; still and all, he was a game fool, not that the thugs he was supposed to be bossing would take that into consideration.

The concertina music, a lively Irish jig, faltered and stopped when Spencer walked through, followed by Lassiter and Callaway. Fingering the buttons quickly, the grinning concertina player, a Cajun swamp-trotter by the look of him, played the opening part of "Here Comes The Bride," using only the high notes. The real hard-cases, and there were plenty of those, brayed like a bunch of jackasses; the others grinned and dug each other with their elbows.

Carpenters had turned the cargo hold into a steel-walled bunkhouse. The three-level bunks lined the bulkheads on both sides of the hold. At the far end there was a rack for guns and other belongings. The hatch covers overhead were open, but the big room stank of tobacco and whisky and sweat. Short of a hurricane or a tidal wave, Lassiter decided to sleep on deck.

Two plug-ugly Irishmen with hard hats were standing in the middle of the floor. Both had bottles, and even with Spencer there they started arguing again about which man could drink the most and dance the longest.

"Quiet, men," Spencer said, trying to roughen up his voice. "I said quiet."

More grinning and elbow digging went on, and Lassiter saw that Mr. Spencer was doing it all wrong. One of the hard-hatted Irishmen turned to the other. A moment before they had been ready to kill one another with broken bottles. Now, facing the young dude, they were friends again. "I cannot understand the man," the first clodhopper said.

"Is he English or what?" his friend said.

Spencer, still cool enough, wanted to know where Axel Norstad was.

"Yo!" a heavy voice answered, and when the circle of men around the dance floor opened up, Lassiter saw a big Swede lying in a lower bunk with his hands clasped behind his head. Norstad looked dumb and kind of happy; filled to the gizzard with whisky and not wanting to be disturbed. The wide grin on the Swede's rawboned face didn't mean a thing to Lassiter; one look told him that Norstad

44

was the toughest son of a bitch in that whole bunch of company thugs.

"Have a drink, cap," Norstad told Spencer, at the same time reaching for a bottle that had gotten away from him. In the steel bunkhouse there was enough whisky to float a canoe, but Norstad's bottle was empty, and that wiped the grin off his face like a schoolteacher erasing figures from a blackboard.

Norstad tossed the bottle and it broke on the metal floor. Spencer had said he didn't want a drink. Sinking into that dangerous bad humor that most drunk Swedes get into sooner or later, Norstad put his hands back behind his head and closed his eyes. He opened them for a moment and looked sourly at Spencer. "You go to hell, mister," he said.

Lassiter knew that Spencer was carrying a shoulder-holstered gun, but he wondered if the dude knew how to use it. The commodore's second-in-command, so called, looked to be the kind of mon-eyed dude that was good at sitting English saddles and shooting targets.

Norstad didn't answer when Spencer told him to get the hell out of that bunk. Spencer's voice had a shake in it; he wasn't scared, just unsure of himself, and that made him mad. "Get up, Norstad. I'm giving you an order. You're supposed to be keeping these men in line—now look at you!"

Norstad flopped his backside against the bottom of the bunk and groaned like a man bothered by fools. A bad taste in his mouth was giving him trouble, and he aimed for Spencer's polished boots when he spat. He licked his lips, displaying broken yellow teeth. Then he raised his close-cropped blond bullet head and glared at Lassiter. Norstad's hair was so short and white-blond that it looked painted onto his hard skull.

"I don't know you, mister cowboy," he told Lassiter in that slow Swede voice. "I don't hire you for this trip—you get out quick."

Lassiter saw no reason not to grin. "Be nice, Axel," he said.

Spencer told Lassiter to keep out of it. "I'll handle this."

"You don't handle nothing, mister." Swinging his thick legs over the side of the bunk, Norstad stood up, and when he was all the way up he was two or three inches over six feet. He wasn't wearing a gun.

Spencer peeled off his coat and handed it to Lassiter. Then he yanked a short-barreled .44 Remington double-action from the shoulder holster and handed that over. Lassiter gave the coat to Callaway, but kept the gun. He thought Spencer would do better to keep the gun, but that was the dude's business. His business and, most likely, his funeral.

"Come on, I'm waiting," Spencer said, raising his fists in John L. style. Just looking at Spencer made Lassiter a little tired. The dude was in good shape, probably kept trim by rowing and fencing, but there wasn't enough weight in the shoulders, not enough meanness in the head, to go up against a saloon fighter like Norstad.

Spencer and his gentlemanly boxing stance seemed to restore the Swede's good humor. He spat on his large-knuckled red hands and rubbed them together like a farmer starting on a pile of wood. Norstad and Spencer were a right interesting pair; the Swede sweating booze through his dirty red-flannel undershirt, the dude in a white linen shirt that

46

some slavey had boiled and ironed.

Spencer stood his ground as the Swede moved in. "Ain't he pretty, boys," Norstad said, jollying his drunken pals.

Spencer told him to fight or shut up. "You'll take orders from me or—"

Norstad's long arm shot forward like a striking rattler. Spencer blocked it, but the force of the blow pushed him back. The Swede yelled and came after him flailing like a windmill, taking Spencer's fast, too-light punches without shifting the wild grin from his face. The Swede didn't have the smallest bit of style: he moved forward flat-footed, taking blows to the head and body, and it didn't even shake him.

Lassiter and Callaway moved out of the way; it was still Spencer's business. A trickle of blood showed at the corners of Norstad's mouth. He sucked back the blood, then spat it in Spencer's face. His next punch went through Spencer's guard and broke his nose. It snapped like a twig; the sound came clear and sharp through the whispering and the heavy breathing of the spectators. Norstad hit Spencer with a right and a left, bringing them in from the side in short, swinging blows. Suddenly dropping his fists, he got Spencer in the belly with a punch that must have pushed his guts up against his backbone. With blood still spraying from his shattered nose, Spencer doubled up like a jackknife. He would have fallen if the Swede hadn't lifted him with another punch brought up from close to the floor. This time Spencer went down and lay motionless in a spreading pool of blood.

So much for amateur prizefighters, Lassiter thought.

But the Swede wasn't ready to end it there. A few white blotches showed on his red face, but for all they bothered him, they might have been put there by an angry girl. Bending quickly, he grabbed the back of Spencer's neck with one powerful hand. "On your feet, mister, you don't get off that easy." He was powerful enough to have lifted Spencer with just one hand; he started to do it.

"Show him who's boss, Axel," the concertina player said.

"Let go," Lassiter said, moving forward. Callaway dropped Spencer's coat and took a step forward. Lassiter said it again. "Back off, Swede."

Norstad was a born show-off. Lassiter didn't see why he didn't join up with a traveling carnival. The rubes would go wild watching him bending spikes and tearing law books in two. The fight with Spencer hadn't even made a dent in him; he was ready and eager to go again.

He let go and Spencer's forehead hit the metal floor. "You want some too, mister?"

Lassiter said no. "Just back off and let that man alone." Norstad was a dirty vicious son of a bitch, but teaching manners to Swedes wasn't what he had been hired to do.

Norstad, grinning hard, appealed to his friends. "The man says no, and that ain't right, that ain't sociable." Turning back to face Lassiter, he said what Lassiter hoped he wouldn't say. "You say No, I say Yes. I'm going to kick a lung out of you, mister."

"Right, boys," he said, turning his head.

That was a mistake. Lassiter drew his gun and belted Norstad across the thick band of muscle where the neck joins the body. He hit him three

times in the same place, putting all his weight behind the blows. Norstad fell down, and behind him
Lassiter heard the hammer on Callaway's '73 Colt
going back.

"Who's next for a haircut?" Lassiter was open for
business. "Step up—no waiting," he said.

Chapter Four

Lassiter pulled Spencer's gun from the waistband of his pants and cocked it. Now both guns were cocked and ready to kill or maim, depending on how hard or easy the Swede's pals wanted to make it. Flat on his face beside Spencer, the Swede began to snore.

"See, he likes it, so don't be bashful, boys." Lassiter moved the guns around to show them that he wasn't playing favorites. "The first man that moves can go to sleep for good."

It seemed like nobody wanted to do that, but one of the dancing Irishman had to say something. Irishmen usually did. "Who in hell are you, mister?"

Lassiter thought about the situation for a minute and decided—why not? Like it or not, they were all in this together, and there might come a time when he'd have to depend on these ugly sons of bitches to back him up. So they might as well get used to taking orders—his orders.

He grinned at the Irishman, the cocked guns

steady in his hands. "I guess I'm your new boss, paddy," he said.

The Irishman shrugged and that seemed to be good enough for the rest of them.

Lassiter put his guns away. "Party's over, boys. The whisky goes over the side. If I catch a man with whisky after we sail, then he goes over the side. Don't look so mournful. Lots of mescal, lots of girls down where we're going."

He knew a good many of them wouldn't ever get to do any drinking or raping. That was fine with him: the world would be better off without them. Him too, he guessed. He grinned at the thought.

Callaway took the feet; together they carried Spencer to his cabin one door down from the commodore's. Callaway went ashore to one of the fish houses and came back with broken ice wrapped in a towel. Spencer's gear was stowed away under his bunk, and after looking through it, Lassiter dug out a silver flask filled with brandy. He pried open Spencer's teeth with his thumb and let some of the brandy trickle through. Lassiter took a swallow himself, then remembered that he never had liked brandy no matter how good or bad it was.

Spencer started to groan when Callaway fetched hot water to wash the blood away. "Got to do it, brother," Callaway said, pushing Spencer's hand away.

Trying to raise himself, Spencer said, "God, I feel all broken up inside."

"Don't think so, no blood coming up." Callaway, looking like an ugly old midwife, finished washing off the blood. The ice in the towel wasn't crushed fine enough, and he slammed it against the side of the bunk. "This is going to hurt like hell for a minute, but it'll ease the pain and bring the swelling down. We ain't sailed yet. Maybe you ought to go ashore and see a doctor. A doctor could do something about that nose. Put some shape back in it, I mean."

Spencer asked Lassiter for another drink of brandy, and he shuddered when it went down. "I was saving that for the battlefield," he said.

"You started the battle early." Lassiter took the bottle back and forced himself to drink. Brandy was sweet, heavy tasting on the tongue, but it had a right pleasant glow when you got it down.

Gallaway had shaped the damp, ice filled towel into a V. "Hold still, brother, here we go."

"Oh Christ!"

Lassiter gave Spencer another drink.

Spencer, looking like a horse with the feedbag on, asked Lassiter what he thought.

Grinning, Lassiter spoke the truth. "Your friend the Swede said you looked pretty. He was right, but now he's wrong. If you want to be pretty again you better do like Callaway says—go ashore."

Spencer said not a chance, and he seemed to have forgotten the fight with Norstad until Lassiter mentioned the Swede's name. "Didn't do very well, did I?"

Topside the steam hooter wailed and they heard the mate yelling Scotch curses. A thumping sound followed by engine vibrations caused the steamer to shudder; the crash of churned-up water came through the open porthole.

"There she goes," Callaway said.

"Anyway who wants to be pretty?" Spencer,

though he said it, didn't sound so sure.

"I think it's an improvement." Lassiter meant it. Everybody had to have his nose broken at least once in his life. "You did all right, considering."

"Considering what?"

"That you acted like a foolish kid, that you didn't have sense enough to kick Norstad in the knackers or go for his eyes or hold a gun on him, make him clean your boots with his tongue. Never get down in the dirt with enlisted men, general. I just broke the Swede back to the ranks—that all right with you?"

"You what?"

"With this." Lassiter touched the butt of his gun. "Not Marquis of Queensberry like you, but it works."

"You mean you killed him?" Even with the ice-pack covering most of his face Spencer's outrage came through.

"Hell no, general. Me kill the best man on board besides myself?"

Callaway, without the ghost of a smile, said Lassiter was not a humble man. "The Swede was getting set to bloody you up some more. Lassiter beat him over the head."

"The neck, brother. The head would be a waste of time."

Spencer said Norstad would have to go. He tried to get up, but Callaway pushed him back onto the bunk. "I don't mean because he bested me." Spencer sounded so God damned sincere. "But I can't have him on board. Call the captain. How can I maintain discipline with the men knowing that Norstad . . ."

"Norstad's a good man," Lassiter said, knowing

there would be more trouble with the Swede, and not caring about it. "Listen, general, some of those so-called hard-cases may look tough to you. Sure they're mean and maybe some are tough, but bouncing in saloons and breaking strikes and breaking heads isn't the best kind of training for fighting Mexican bandits. Believe you me, the Swede is the genuine article. We need men like him."

Callaway chimed in with: "Norstad's as bad as they come--and I ought to know. Now you take another drink and try to get some sleep. You'll be feeling fine by the time we clear Grand Island."

Spencer took Callaway's advice; this time he was able to hold the brandy flask himself. After that he closed his eyes and his voice got slow and sleepy. "Thank you, both of you . . ."

Though he had gone to sleep they both answered. Callaway, poker faced, said the young dude was entirely welcome.

Lassiter told Spencer to save his thanks. So far as he was concerned, the dude and his damn-fool gentlemanly ways could go straight to hell. He had stopped the Swede from killing the kid, but he would have done as much for the smelliest rumpot on the New Orleans docks. Lassiter had no use for the Swede, but when he came right down to it, he was more Norstad's kind of people than he was Spencer's.

He went topside to walk the prison stiffness out of his legs, to breathe in clean air, to get rid of the big city stink. Getting clear of the shipping in the harbor, the *Judah P. Benjamin* began to pick up speed. He could tell that by the night wind in his face, by the spray breaking across the bow, by the way the sound of the engines changed. He would have given a lot to be heading back west to Texas, instead of into the God-blasted Gulf of Mexico, but he knew he couldn't go back to Texas until he killed Betancourt, or somebody else did for the sneaking bastard. Rolling and lighting a cigarette, he decided he wasn't all that mad at the doublecrosser. In fact, now that he was long gone from the Parish Prison, he wasn't mad at all. Betancourt had pulled a doublecross, and a man had to expect that. Just as Betancourt had to expect that he'd be coming after him. Killing the doublecrosser was something he had to do, a matter of business, so to speak.

He walked down the deck where some of the hard-cases had collected whisky bottles in a sack and were dumping them over the side. The two Irishmen were there and they couldn't have looked more down-in-the-mouth if the order had been to dump their sainted mothers.

Most of the booze had gone over by the time Lassiter got there; the hard-cases turned around when they heard him coming. Everything but one full, corked bottle had gone into the sea, and the Irishman holding that last live soldier held it up to the light, turning it this way and that.

"Better get rid of it, Jem," the other Irishman was saying when Lassiter reached the sad scene.

"A bloody awful shame," his friend said, and got ready to throw the bottle.

Lassiter stopped him. "Not that way—this way, paddy."

"But you said, sir."

"Different rules for you and me, paddy."

"Is there no justice in the world, sir?" The Irishman knew the answer, but he asked anyway.

"I guess not," Lassiter decided, hefting the bottle in his hand. He knew he could get whisky some place on the ship, but he wanted to make a point. A man couldn't make his points too often with this bunch of bruisers.

"I'm sorry to hear you say that, sir."

Lassiter had made one point; to make another he gave the bottle to the Irishman and told him to take a drink. "Everyone take a small drink," he said.

They passed the bottle around, then gave it back; about half the quart was gone.

"See how it works, boys," Lassiter said. "The Lord giveth and the Lord taketh away. So do I."

"God bless you, sir," the Irishman called Jem declared. "You're a scholar and a . . ."

Lassiter told him to go to hell, and walked away with the bottle.

Sometime later the *Judah P. Benjamin* passed Grand Island, off on the port side, and headed out into the Gulf. It had been cool in New Orleans, but the night wind rushing over the steamer warmed up as they passed the north tip of the strung-out chain of rocks called the Chandleur Islands. After that the course was southeast through the Yucatan Channel; past there they would steer south and west along the far side of Quintana Roo.

Standing at the ship's rail, smoking and taking short drinks from the bottle, Lassiter listened to the captain giving orders to the first mate. The wind was coming in from the sea; it was heavy with salt and spray. After the captain finished yelling and

59

went below, it was quiet except for the thud of the engines and the crash of white water against the bow.

Lassiter freed a corner of the tarpaulin covering one of the steam launches, put the whisky bottle inside, then went below to get a blanket and to see how Spencer was.

Callaway was sitting in a chair beside the bunk. "Still asleep," Callaway said. "Norstad's awake and sober, came over to inquire after the boy. That Swede thinks you done him dirt."

"He's right," Lassiter agreed.

He found a blanket and took it back to the launch. It was early and still warm; later in the night it would get colder. Wrapped up good, he smoked and drank for a while before he went to sleep. Just before he closed his eyes he wondered where Betancourt was.

Sometime during the night it rained; rain splashing on the tarpaulin woke him. He listened to the ship's bell ringing the hours. From time to time some hard-case came topside and emptied his guts over the rail into the sea. Lassiter grinned and went back to sleep.

When he woke again it was close to dawn; the sun was a burning ball of fire inching up over the horizon. The sea was calm, red instead of blue; the only thing that hadn't changed was the steady thud of the engines.

Lassiter felt hungry.

Chapter Five

Making three hundred miles a day, the *Judah P. Benjamin* had good weather and a calm sea all the way southeast to the Yucatan Channel. Long before they crossed the Tropic of Cancer a man could burn his hand touching metal on deck. The sun beat down on the ship, putting tempers on edge, and even the salt spray was warm by the time it reached their faces.

By the time they went through the Yucatan Channel, the commodore had stopped coming out of his cabin to give his brief but hearty talks to the men. Commodore Ruffin had packed a lot of ice on board, but not enough sawdust had been used to keep it from melting; two days out of New Orleans there was nothing left but a pile of damp sawdust. The men were edgy. Lassiter wasn't edgy—just fed up with being cooped up in too small a space. Callaway slept a good part of the time; when he wasn't asleep he read his Bible—Bender's Bible.

The next day they were steering a westerly course

along the south coast of Quintana Roo. A day back from the entrance to the Yucatan Gulf the other company ship, the *Lafayette,* had dropped off behind them.

It was at least as hot as hell or Death Valley at noon in July, and Lassiter was on deck hunkered down in what shade he could find, when Spencer came topside and said the commodore wanted to hold a meeting in his cabin. "It looks like we're really here," Spencer said. The broken nose had partways healed; it sprawled all over his face and made him look tougher and older; his face didn't fit with the excitement in his voice.

Lassiter gave the dude a sour grin. "How many derricks you figure to use to get the commodore ashore?"

Having his nose broken and other things had made some changes in Spencer; to Lassiter he was still a stiff-necked jackass with more money than was good for him. "The commodore's all right," Spencer said. "Anyway he's my uncle in case you didn't know."

Lassiter said he didn't know, didn't care, but he followed Spencer below to the fat man's cabin. The commodore had his own bathtub on board, but the cabin smelled of the fat old man, and maybe the commodore wasn't nearly so brave, now that every thud of the ship's engines carried him closer to Sandoval.

For a change, the commodore wasn't stuffing his gut with food when they got there, but he had been doing that not long before. A napkin big enough to wrap a baby in flopped down from his collar, and the wine bottle on the desk had been punished within an inch of its life. And that wasn't the first bottle, because when the commodore spoke he sounded as if he might be gargling with molasses.

"Ah, Lassiter," he said. "Glad to have you with us."

Lassiter said he'd been on board all the time. He said that, then asked why Norstad wasn't there. "The Swede should hear all this," he said.

The commodore didn't think that was necessary, but in the end Callaway was sent to fetch the Swede.

"Lassiter's right," Spencer said.

"Is he now?" Commodore Ruffin looked as if he'd rather be sailing in the Long Island Sound. He helped himself to a glass of wine, smacked his lips, then fumbled in the desk for a map. "Here we are, gentlemen," he said. He moved a fat finger across the paper. "And there is the enemy—where we hope the enemy is. And here . . ."

Callaway came in with the Swede; Norstad stood by himself, doing nothing, saying nothing, not looking directly at anyone.

The commodore got back to business, moving the map around so they could see it from the other side of the desk. Tapping the paper again, the commodore said, "Here marked, marked here is the city of Santa Clara, a walled city, a Spanish stronghold build in the late seventeenth century, Mr. Spencer assures me."

He looked at Spencer and got a nod.

"Jesus Christ," Lassiter thought.

"Sandoval may have re-fortified Santa Clara"—Commodore Ruffin laughed at the idea—"using the original cannon. Nothing is beyond these Mexicans.

Cannon aside, gentlemen, you will be gladdened to learn that in the matter of small arms, this Sandoval has nothing more lethal than smooth-bore muskets left over from the time of Maximilian . . ."

"When do we go in?" Lassiter interrupted the commodore's flow of useless words.

"Impatient to lock horns, eh." Commodore Ruffin's paunch rose and fell; he was laughing. "First thing in the morning, my good man. Captain Dunnock assures me that we'll come abreast of Santa Clara sometime late this very night."

"Yeah," Lassiter said.

The commodore smiled at him. "But we won't attack Santa Clara. Certainly fifty men with repeating rifles could take the city—it's a very small city—but we won't do that, because that's what they'll be expecting."

Norstad spoke for the first time. "Why not, mister? "You say it can be done. This Swede use to be a sailor. I have sailed this coast. Santa Clara is the place to land. Other places are bad—the currents. That's why the Spanish built Santa Clara where they did."

The commodore told the Swede to hold his tongue. "Makes no difference to me, I don't care," Norstad said.

"I said hold your tongue."

The Swede didn't display his hands palms upward like an Italian; the shrug he gave was the same. He shut his mouth and didn't say anything else for the rest of the meeting.

Lassiter hadn't made any protest, but the commodore pointed a finger at him. "You're here on someone else's business." The finger swung arund to

66

point at Callaway. "So is this man. Therefore, I'll thank you not to interfere with my plans."

Shuffling the map around, the commodore moved his fat finger along the coast of Quintana Roo. "Better to make a landing east of Santa Clara, the current's not so treacherous, the surf not so strong. We won't do that either. No, gentlemen, we won't do that. West of the city, where it's hard to land—we'll land there. At the place where we're least expected. Outfox the greasy brigands, that's what we'll do. Strategy, in a word."

Lassiter could feel Lee, Grant, Sherman turning over in their graves.

"Any further argument?" Commodore Ruffin made it clear that argument was the last thing he wanted. He wanted cheers but got none from Lassiter, Callaway, the sullen Swede. His nephew offered some faint praise: "If you're right, Uncle, we'll sweep ashore like a sharp scythe."

"I'm always right, boy," Commodore Ruffin declared.

Morning came up bright and red and beautiful, the sea haze and the heat thinned by a strong breeze coming in from the Caribbean. Lassiter had pulled on his boots and checked his weapons long before first light. He finished a third mug of coffee and went topside, where Spencer had the men lined up along the ship's rail.

Up on the bridge with the captain, Commodore Ruffin was scanning the long low coastline with a big brass telescope. The steamer was about a mile offshore, and in the bright clear morning air Lassiter didn't need any spy glass.

"Uncover the launches," the Scotch captain yelled to the first mate. The order was passed on to the crew, and there was a sudden flurry of activity on the silent ship.

"Get ready to lower away," the captain shouted next.

Lassiter took a last drag on his cigarette and sent the stub spinning into the sea before he climbed into one of the three steam launches. Spencer was in charge of the first launch; Norstad was giving orders in the second; Lassiter was bossing the third.

"Take them up," the captain called from the bridge. The commodore, puffing hard, was the last man to climb into the launches. The old man clapped his nephew on the shoulder. Everybody else —leaving out the sailors that manned the boats— was wearing crossed bandoliers, every last loop filled with .44-40 shells for the Winchesters; only the commodore had a sword. Lassiter grinned sourly. It was a real fancy sword with a long straight blade and a silver chased guard; just the kind of thing to hang on a wall for people to admire. Out there in that stinking jungle it wouldn't do the commodore a bit of good.

The derricks were worked by small steam-powered engines, and when the captain's order was passed along, the thick tarred ropes whined as the drum began to turn. Spencer's boat was lowered first; it went up high, then swung out over the rail. It came down easily in the sea, and the crewmen used oars to push it away from the steamer. The engine came to life with a muffled puttering sound, and the first launch moved away from the ship.

Lassiter used the few minutes of waiting to check his men for arms and equipment: rifle, bandoliers, machete, canteen, handgun. Each launch had a small supply of food that wouldn't rot in the heat: jerked meat, hard biscuits, dried apples. What food they carried wouldn't go past the second day; after that they were to travel light and live off the country.

"Hang on, here we go," Lassiter said. They went up and over and down into the sea. The wind from the sea was blowing harder, and the crewmen had to fight hard with the oars to keep the last launch from being pulled in by the roll of the ship. Then the engine, gaining power, pushed the launch away from the ship, but the heavily loaded boat dipped and lurched as the sea grew rougher and the spray broke over the bow, soaking crew and passengers with salt water.

Up ahead the wind-whipped surf crashed heavily on the beach. Spencer's and Norstad's launches had slowed their engines, so they could all hit the beach at the same time. Nothing moved on the long stretch of sand between the water and the edge of the bright green jungle. East of where they were, maybe a mile away, the walled city of Santa Clara jutted up tall and hard in the morning sun, and at full tide the sea washed against the thick stone walls of the fort. After three hundred years of pounding by the sea the walls hadn't budged an inch, and when the northers came the sea washed across the sand, leaving the town like a ship afloat.

Lassiter had no spy glass, but the town looked to be as empty as the beach and the jungle. Maybe Sandoval and his rebels had all gone fishing; Lassiter didn't believe it for a minute. He looked over at Spencer's boat and saw the commodore waving his damn-fool sword. Spencer waved, so did Norstad. "All right—now," Lassiter told the man at the tiller.

"Judas Priest," Callaway said poking the air with his rifle. Lassiter had seen them at the same time. Back of the beach the sand hills opened in a V, and through it a column of horsemen was riding fast, the sun glinting on their fancy trappings. They were still about eight hundred yards away, but once they got through to the flat, packed sand of the beach they would close the gap in minutes.

"Full throttle," Lassiter ordered the engine man. "Crash on through, the hell with the launch." He knew the repeating rifles wouldn't make any difference against smoothbore carbines if Sandoval's men trapped them in the surf.

He pulled his belt-gun and stuck it in his pants pocket, took a good hold on the Winchester and got ready to jump. The launch, with the steam engine opened out all the way, hit the surf like a locomotive running off the tracks. The launch was thick-timbered and heavy, but the surf picked it up and tossed it like a dead tree rolling down a canyon in a flash flood. Then suddenly it broke through, the froth-topped waves lifting it, pushing it from behind; the beach came rushing at them. "Jump! Get out before it hits," Lassiter yelled. Holding the rifle high, he jumped after Callaway. A wave hit him from behind like a sack of spuds and sent him staggering. He went down on his knees in the hissing water; the launch roared past him with men jumping and yelling. Some were yelling, still trying to jump off when the prow of the launch knifed into solid wet sand and broke like matchwood. Two men broke up with the boat. One of the dancing Irishmen got a shattered spike of wood through his belly, and lay there screaming in the wreckage of the launch with the surf washing over him. Lassiter didn't know what the other man was. He was dead with a gaping head wound through which blood and brains oozed like boiled-over milk pudding. Lassiter turned the Winchester, jacked a shell and put the dying Irishman out of his misery. Pulled back out into the surf another man was yelling for help. The current pulled him under and he didn't come up again.

Pushing and cursing, Lassiter got ten or twelve men out of the water and down on their bellies in the sand to meet the first wave of the attack. He didn't know how many Mexicans were riding down on them. Fifty mounted men coming fast—maybe more than that. Most of Spencer's men were ashore by now, but Norstad's boat had capsized in the surf, and all Lassiter could hear from that part of the beach was yelling and screaming.

"Get down for Christ's sake," Lassiter roared when Spencer and his men came running to join them. The rebels had spread out and were coming in wide. For the Mexicans the range wasn't good yet, but the men out in front were firing.

"Easy men," Spencer said, wild eyed and dripping.

"Bullshit—open fire," Lassiter roared, up on one knee, swinging the barrel of the Winchester to get his first Mexican. It was easy shooting, but there sure as hell were a lot of fellas in big hats. Jacking shells fast and steady, he started from the left side and knocked four men out of their saddles before he swung the rifle barrel from the jungle back to the sea. A musket ball fanned the side of his face and killed the man behind him. The Mexican who fired was one of those fellas you see in every battle; lay down the heaviest fire and somehow they ride through. Southerners and Apaches and some Mexicans were like that. Like hell he was! That Mexican thought he was the Angel of Death and he wasn't more than thirty feet from breaking through their line when Lassiter shot him twice in the chest.

The Mexicans came on fast and wild, howling like drunken Indians and ready to die; they had the courage and the numbers, but their short old-fashioned cavalry carbines and sabers were no match for the quick-firing Winchesters. Gun-spooked horses ran through the line of shooters—but no men. Lassiter lay on his side reloading the Winchester. Something flopped in the sand between him and Callaway. It was short and fat, and it wheezed like a punctured big bladder.

"How do you like them apples?" Lassiter asked Commodore Ruffin.

He lined up the rifle barrel to start firing again, and then he saw Betancourt coming right at him in the last wave of the charge. Even through the hell of gunsmoke and kicked-up sand there was no mistaking the doublecrossing son of a bitch. Betancourt wore some kind of gaudy Mex uniform with a floppy sombrero riding low on his face, but Lassiter recognized the man he had come so far to kill. Yelling and cursing in Spanish, he was telling his men to fall back, fall back, but his men were Mexicans and the killing mood was on them. Betancourt rode after them, a brace of plated .45 Colts in his hands. He kept telling his riders to fall back.

Lassiter cursed when they started to do it, not because of orders: the fire from the line of Winchesters was too deadly even for them. Still cursing, Lassiter stood up straight, though the retreating Mexicans were turning, reloading their short muskets in the saddle, and laying out a scattered but fairly heavy fire.

Horses and men got between Lassiter and Betancourt, and some rode out of the way and others were downed by bullets. Lassiter spotted Betancourt again and started shooting at him as fast as he could work the lever, but the range was long for a saddle gun, and when the hammer of the Winchester clicked on nothing, Betancourt was still on his horse, still yelling.

Throwing down his rifle, Lassiter pulled his belt gun and yelled, "Betancourt, you greasy son of a bitch," hoping to draw him in with insults. He had to shout himself raw in the throat before Betancourt heard him. Lassiter saw his hand go up to push back the sombrero. Betancourt swept off his big hat and waved before he put the spurs to his black Arabian and rode off after what was left of his retreating cavalry.

Callaway stood up slapping dried salt and sand from his clothes. The rest of the men were pretty cocky after turning back the Mexicans, but Callaway had the dead calm of a mild man nagged for thirty years by a shrill wife he can't shake loose. "So that's what he looks like," he said to Lassiter.

Lassiter told him to go find a sheep.

Chapter Six

After they finished counting the dead and killing the wounded that couldn't be moved, they moved away from the beach and into the edge of the jungle. Seven of the men from the capsized launch were still missing, and that meant they were battered to death or killed by drowning. Six men were killed during the attack; five wounded; of those five three had to be shot.

Spencer turned his head and walked away when Lassiter told Norstad and Callaway to take care of it. They did it quickly and Lassiter saw Spencer's body twitch as the three shots rang out.

Lassiter followed Spencer into the shelter of the trees, but before they got there, the commodore came running into the open with the same damn-fool sword in his hand. The blade was snapped off in the middle; the commodore, blotch-faced with fear, didn't seem to notice. Lassiter thought it was a pity the top half of the sword wasn't buried in the commodore's bloated belly. Offshore the *Judah P. Ben-*

jamin sounded its hooter and the thud of its engines was carried in on the wind. Commodore Ruffin ran past pulling at Spencer's arm. "No, no, we must send a signal. Tell them to wait, Spencer. It's no good, I tell you."

Spencer went after the old man and stopped him. "Too late, uncle," he said. "Dunnock can't get us off now—the boats are done for."

"So are we if we don't get away from here," Lassiter said. "Dunnock's the smart one in this party."

Lassiter went into the jungle where the men were waiting and started his count. He came up with thirty-two, and that seemed to be right.

Helping the commodore through the sand slowed Spencer; he let the old man slide and asked Lassiter how bad it was.

Lassiter said "Bad enough. Eighteen dead, more than a third." He spat in the direction of the commodore, who was lying against a tree, his chest heaving in the heat. "What next, general?"

"Dunnock and the *Benjamin* will be back." Spencer didn't sound too convinced.

"So will the Mexicans." Lassiter didn't have a doubt in the world that they would.

"We beat them back the first time. We'll do it again."

"Maybe the second time too—not the third. My guess is they were spread thin north and south of Santa Clara before the first attack. Maybe the commodore was right—they didn't expect us to land where we did, but they got here faster than he thought. Christ, sonny, why didn't somebody say this was a real war instead of a bunch of bandits. Your friends sent a hundred men to put down a genuine rebellion."

"Sandoval is a bandit." Spencer didn't want to have his mind changed.

The sun, climbing higher in the sky, was soaking steam out of the tangled jungle growth. A hairy black spider ran up a tree and one of the men jerked his pistol and fired at it. He missed and the spider took itself out of danger.

Lassiter faced the man who shot and told him to put his gun away. The shooter was the concertina-playing Cajun with the sense of humor. Lassiter was just about sick of this so-called expedition. "That's a spider, Frenchy," he said. "A spider and not a Mexican. Look hard the next spider you see—they don't wear big hats."

"Well, what do you think?" Spencer was ready to take some advice. "Do we stay or go?"

"You make it sound so easy, sonny."

"That's the second time you called me that. Don't do it again."

Lassiter started to tell Spencer what he could do with his orders. He stopped and grinned at the smash-nosed dude. "It's a deal, *Mister* Spencer. That doesn't mean you're not a fool."

The young dude puffed up again.

"Like me," Lassiter said, going on with it. "Your Scotchman will be back, when I don't know, and you don't know. Maybe he'll sail north and meet up with the *Lafayette* and bring men from there. Don't mean to be gloom-faced, but they could be having the same kind of trouble we're having."

"You are gloom-faced," Spencer told Lassiter.

"Not yet. What we need is horses. We get our-selves horses we can ride up into Yucatan or the other way to Campeche. I say Campeche—more likely to be Mex soldiers there, Rurales too. Sandoval won't be busting his britches to tangle with those boys."

"That's about a hundred miles either way we decide."

"That's why we need horses."

"Where do you figure to find them?"

Lassiter waved his in a westerly direction. "Best as I can recall, this country isn't all jungle. Good cattle and horse country beyond there, they tell me."

Callaway was lying close-by with his eyes closed, but Lassiter knew the sheep-faced man catcher wasn't asleep. Opening his droopy eyelids, Callaway said, "What about your friend from Natchez?"

Lassiter had no doubts that Betancourt would manage to follow along. He was counting on that, and that was what he told Callaway. Getting back to the horses, he said they didn't need all the men; a few good men could get mounts for all of them—or they'd all die in Quintana Roo.

The sun was up in the full blaze of noon before they got ready to move out: Spencer, Callaway, the surviving jig-time Irishman named Kinsella, who said he'd been in the British lancers in India; Norstad, a Dane who gave his name as Rasmussen—and Lassiter. Listening to Lassiter, Spencer put the Cajun—nobody called him by any other name—in charge of the party in the jungle. The Cajun might be jittery about poisonous spiders—brought up in swamp country as he had been—but he still looked to be a fair sample of a man.

"Watch the jungle, not the beach," Lassiter

warned the Louisiana Frenchman before they eased away from their position. "And if the Scotchman changes his mind and comes back with the *Benjamin*—go with him. Try to."

Commodore Ruffin, lying heavily against the bottom of a moss covered tree, stopped grunting and woke up in time to see them off. An empty silver brandy just like his nephew's slid from the sleeve of his now dirty uniform and fell beside him in the moss without making a sound. The cork stopper hung loose from the flask, so Lassiter knew the old man had been cheating. Norstad and Callaway had shot wounded men who could have used a last drink of brandy before they took a bullet in the head. Lassiter didn't give a good God damn about the wounded men they had to kill; still, bad or good—and most were bad—they could have used some of that brandy to make their passing easier. He rolled his tongue around his mouth and spat. He couldn't recall any job that made him spit as much as this one.

Holding onto the tree, Spencer's fat uncle stood up on shaking legs, saying: "God go with us, lads."

Spencer told his uncle goodbye with a wave.

Callaway liked the old man's farewell. "And with you too, brother," he replied.

Lassiter just spat. He knew he'd have to remember not to spit so often in such hot country. Fragments of this or that thought came to him: Frank Bender maybe eating a big dinner in Brennan's in the French Quarter; that wild Honduran girl in Madame Gertie's; the Palace of Perfect Pleasure Saloon in El Paso. More than ever he wanted to kill friend Betancourt. He wasn't mad—just eager.

The best way to go—the only way they figured how to go—was to move out onto the beach and walk in Indian file to the place where Betancourt and his cavalry had come through the V in the sand hills. It wasn't like Callaway to say something when he hadn't been asked a question. They were up high on the beach, close to the jungle where the sand was dry and drifted loosely like snow. "Lordy, but I could use a sturdy Texas cow pony along about now," Callaway said.

Norstad, no horseman, had the right answer. "Wouldn't last a day in this heat, mister. That's why we don't bring no horse this trip."

Lassiter told them to button their mouths. Betancourt and his riders had gone back in the direction of Santa Clara. That didn't mean they hadn't eased out, a small detachment, and weren't waiting on both sides of the break in the sand hills. "You're moving out too far into the open," he warned Spencer. "Probably they won't be too organized after the beating they took—we'd better slide in here still it gets close to dark. No talking—we listen."

Some time later, much later, Spencer shook Lassiter's arm. "It's getting dark."

Lassiter had slept for an hour while the sun was up; he'd been awake, his eyes closed, for three hours. On a job like this keeping his face blank and his eyes closed was the only way to get away from fools and their talk.

He sat up. "Glad you noticed that."

"Shit!" It was the only time *Mister* Spencer had fouled his mouth with a dirty word. So Lassiter grinned.

The sun had moved west, and now they couldn't see it because it was on the other side of the high wall of jungle, but its dying red light changed the colors of the sea and the beach. It turned the jungle from bright green to dark green, but no matter what color the jungle was it still smelled of rot and fever and dying things. Lassiter was used to the sun-blasted—the bare, dry, rocky—spaces of the Southwest. The jungle, this or any other jungle, made him think of rich food that had been left too long on someone's table. It was like brandy: you put up with it when there was nothing else.

"We'll know soon," he said.

Moving slowly, stopping to listen and look, they came to the break in the sand hills, and started through to the other side, and when they were all the way to the other side they stopped to rest.

Lassiter stood up and said, "Well it's not Texas, *Mister* Spencer." Far off there were sharp-spined hills; and you could call them mountains if you had never seen the Rockes. Some jungle grew back from the sand hills; a few miles past that it looked like more forest than jungle. Lassiter knew traveling there would be easier. "How about it, *Mister* Spencer? You got a reading knowledge of this country, the commodore tells me."

Spencer told him to drop the *mister*. "My first name is Fairfax, but my friends call me Jack." He seemed to be ashamed of his given name—with good reason, Lassiter thought.

Lassiter looked at him. "I'll call you Spencer."

Spencer said the forest out there was mostly mahogany and rubber trees, with some dyewoods. It wasn't as open as it looked: most of the way through would be choked with llianas and tree fern. The Mexicans native to the place called it *tierra caliente;* between the sea and the forest the jungle steamed night and day with malaria and crawled with snakes and poisonous spiders. "Not to leave out *El lagarto.*" Spencer said that meant alligator. "Bigger ones than we know."

Lassiter spoke cracked but fluent Mexican Spanish, but he thanked Spencer for the lesson. At first Spencer got huffy, then he grinned.

"What made you so sour, Lassiter?"

"Fellas like you—mostly." Lassiter grinned back. "On your feet, boys."

They hadn't been ambushed coming through the natural place to come through the sand hills, so he told them to spread out and go slow. The best place for an ambush wasn't always where experienced bushwhackers showed up.

They cleared the low hills and started down into the jungle. "Now we make some time," Lassiter said. "We do that, or spend the night with the snakes."

The sun had slid lower in the west, but it wasn't gone yet, and the hills in the distance, the red sun behind them, showed clear red on the near slopes and jagged on the top. "Now's the time to tell us things," Lassiter said to Spencer. "A fella I drank with in a bar in Vera Cruz one time swore they got half-wild colored people living along this coast. You figure them for friendly—or don't you know?"

"Not friendly, not unfriendly," Spencer said, thinking back to the books he'd read at college. He grinned at Lassiter, but they were in deep jungle and it was getting dark; all Lassiter saw was the flash of Spencer's white even teeth underneath his broken nose.

Lassiter said good.

"Not wild either. Anyway, they're not all Negro—none of them. Somehow they got here from the West Indies and mixed in with the Indians. They won't bother us if we don't bother them."

Lassiter asked Spencer how sure he was.

"Sure as Professor Dutcher at Harvard can make me," Spencer answered.

They went the rest of the way without talking. They got through three miles of jungle before the sun dropped down and blanked out the light. About two more miles of jungle was left after that, and they took longer to get through that by the faint moonlight that filtered down through the canopy of green overhead.

"By Crikey, we're through," Kinsella, the Irishman said. It was the only thing he had said for many hours. Except for occasional curses in Danish, Rasmussen hadn't said much, but that could be put down to the fact that he didn't know much English. Axel Norstad knew plenty of English but hadn't said a word.

They bedded down in a clearing between young mahogany trees, and chewed on jerked meat and drank a little water before they went to sleep. It was ten o'clock by Spencer's narrow silver watch. Lassiter said they were five men and would take hourly watches until three the next morning. That way they all got to sleep four hours, and still have two hours traveling time before first light.

"Traveling will be slow but we'll make some distance," he told them. He was still feeling mean for having missed Betancourt with a full load of bullets.

Damn! he thought with his back against a tree while the others dropped off to sleep: he must have been too anxious to kill the doublecrosser. He cursed quietly. That wasn't it—he just plain missed because the range wasn't right. Now with a Big Fifty Sharps he could have blown Betancourt clear out of the saddle. That wasn't just a way of talking: in his time he'd seen one or two men lifted by a Big Fifty.

He listened to night sounds and chewed on a cigarette that he rolled more tightly than usual but didn't light. Once again he wondered where Betancourt was, wondered why Betancourt had bothered to cheat him out of ten thousand when the son of a bitch had forty thousand free and clear as a silver bell.

Betancourt was just plain greedy; and whether for his cause or for himself didn't matter a damn. Lassiter grinned in the darkness. He had come all the way to south Mexico to kill a friend of Senor Sandoval, a friend of the people, as the Mexicans said about every tinhorn rebel or put-upon general who set himself up as the true and only savior of the Republic of Mexico.

Tilting his canteen, Lassiter took a short snort of water, and tasting the warm water and thinking of cold beer back at the Perfect Palace Saloon in El Paso put an extra stab in the throbbing pain behind his eyes. That pain was always there when he was close to killing a man he wanted to kill, had to kill. The pain was like the hunches other men got but he didn't trust himself. He guessed it was something like a hunch. He could have done without the pain though it always went away after he had killed the man he had set out to kill.

Norstad got up to stand his watch without being called.

Chapter Seven

Lassiter didn't sleep for four hours. Kinsella, the Irishman taking the last watch, had Spencer's watch, and said it was two-fifteen. The others slept while Lassiter sat with his back against a tree and chewed on jerked beef until the Irishman looked at the watch again and said it was five minutes till three.

In the sky the moon was still strong at that hour; not much light slanted down to where they were. But there was more light than in the jungle behind them. Spencer was right about the tree fern and llianas, and there were places where they had to chop hard with the machetes to clear the way.

When they stopped to rest about two miles from where they had started that morning, Lassiter said he thought another three miles should take them out of the narrow strip of forest.

Nobody felt like talking, not even the Irishman, and when they walked out of the shade of the trees into the first morning light they were quiet.

"Rest and drink," Lassiter ordered.

After that, still quiet, they moved out into the huge grassy plain that ran all the way from the end of the forest to the distant mountains. It wasn't as flat and open as it looked from miles back; low hills crossed it from east to west; and there were stretches of tangled growth where a small army could hide. Still and all, most of it was flat rich country covered with foot-high waving yellow grass. Lassiter thought it looked something like Minnesota, that is, if Minnesota had been baked for five hundred years by tropical sun.

"There's a good piece of water over yonder," Callaway said, pointing.

Going down the slope, Lassiter had seen the gun-metal streak of water before Callaway had. He nodded and didn't answer. As they went down the incline from the long stretch of forest, a sprawl of chaparral-covered hills cut off the view.

"Well?" The query came from Spencer.

Lassiter said: "In country like this water has to mean ranches or haciendas. That's what it should mean, but you never know about Mexicans. What does Professor Butcher have to say about the subject?"

"Dutcher, not Butcher. You don't like Mexicans very much, do you, Lassiter?"

"I like them better than your uncle."

On the other side of the first ridge there was a Negro-Indian village in a grove of trees; cooking fires sent blue smoke straight up into the motionless air. A dog barked and kept barking long before they reached the cluster of pole and palm huts. Some night streaks were still darkening the sky, but women and girls were already working in patches of yams, chile, melons, calabash. Sprawling about the cook fires with red earthenware dishes of boiled maize at their elbows, the men looked as if they never worked at all. Lassiter decided those fellas had worked out a pretty good system.

Nobody in the village looked surprised to see them. The women kept working with crude hoes, and the men didn't stand up. Lassiter didn't see why every black-brown man in the village needed a machete to eat his breakfast. They were an odd looking bunch; good people to let alone, he decided.

He spoke Border Spanish to the head man, a big fella with a fine head of fuzzy steel-grey hair and one milky eye. The eye gave him a sinister look, but he seemed reasonable enough, and though Lassiter didn't understand all the words in his answer, he understood enough to know they could rest and eat something there before they continued their journey. Old Milky Eye didn't ask where they were going, and without having to say it he made it clear that they had to move on as soon as their bellies were full.

The women brought food and the men got out their long hardwood pipes for the first smoke of the day. An old burro with a shaggy coat wandered into the clearing and began to nibble at a string of red peppers tied to a pole. Smoking solemnly, the black Indians watched the burro as if they had never seen a donkey before. In a few minutes the burro brayed like a broken bugle, kicked up his heels and galloped off looking for water. Everybody smiled and then their dark faces were solemn again.

Lassiter decided the boiled maize wasn't bad if

you dumped on enough wild honey. He ate a cooked green banana and drank water from his canteen. "You sure they don't take sides?" he asked Spencer. The head man's cane cutter looked sharp enough to take a man's head off with one slice."

Spencer shook his head. "I said they don't. You notice they don't ask questions. The Mexicans stay away from them, and the only trouble was back in the Sixties when the French were here. A general named Levesque tried to round them up to build a military road. He never built a mile of road, but he lost an awful lot of men."

Lassiter thanked the head man and made a sign that it was time to move out. The head man acknowledged the thanks with slow nods, but didn't get up. Neither did the rest of them. Figuring they were something like backhome Indians, Lassiter made his only question casual—was this a good country to find horses?

"*Hay muchos, muchisimos,*" (They are many) Milky Eye said, pointing to the open country beyond the village.

That was close enough for Lassiter, and he thanked the head man again.

Another ridge had to be crossed before they made it out to grassy country. Sweating in the fierce heat they came to a small meadow, and at the far end of it a tall knob covered with chaparral stuck up like an Indian burial mound. It was a good place to climb and see what lay beyond—and it was a perfect spot for an ambush.

"You wait here," Lassiter said. "Fifty, a hundred men could be laying for us on that hill—all that cover. Out in the meadow we'd be like ducks."

Spencer said: "What'll you be like?"

"Like a duck, *Mister* Spencer, but you cover me the best you can."

He started across through the thick yellow grass, and there was no wind, no sound except his boots rustling in the grass. Some ground-nesting bird burst from cover in a squawking flurry of wings; it got quiet again, and Lassiter hoped the next sound he heard wouldn't be made by a rifle.

He got to the bottom of the knob without getting killed, and ten minutes later, atop the hill, he turned and could see the Caribbean flashing white and blue in the distance. The other side of the knob ran straight down to a wide plain that ran for miles to the mountains on the far side; far out a narrow thread of water opened into a small lake. Thousands of cattle drifted through the deep grass, and beside the lake was a house behind an orange grove.

Lassiter waved them to come ahead before he started down the other side of the hill. About thirty minutes later, looking back now and then to see how Spencer and the others were doing, he reached the edge of the lake and followed it toward the house, the fat sleek cattle moving slowly out of his way. If a man could get used to the fierce heat, it was about the best cow country he'd ever seen—but where in hell were the owners?

With the Winchester ready to shoot, he went through the orange trees. The air was sweet, heavy, lifeless; he still couldn't get a good look at the house because, beyond the orange grove, a dense hedge of jasmine cut off the view. He stopped when he heard a girl's voice. She spoke in Spanish and another girl answered.

Between the orange grove and the house a channel had been cut in from the lake; the channel ended in a circular basin walled with blue tile; following the circle of the pool was a low parapet of cut stone. Lassiter grinned. The two girls were in the pool, and sun flashed on water when they lifted their arms to move around.

One was blond, one was dark. The dark one was saying, *"Anda!—anda—hace mucho calor. Vamos a volver."* (Hurry up—hurry up—it's hot. Let's get back.)

Holding up something that looked like a goldfish, the blond girl called out: *"Lupe! mira! que bonito."* (Lupe! Look here! What a pretty thing!)

Suddenly Lassiter's face twitched and he jerked the Winchester to his shoulder. A huge alligator, a lot bigger than a Florida gator, was crawling silently over the parapet, dragging its tail through the mud and weeds on the lake side of the pool.

"El cayman!" Lassiter yelled, sighting along the rifle barrel. The two girls turned and screamed as the alligator slithered over the wall and dropped into the pool.

He had to chance hitting the girls. He aimed for the gator's skull and fired; the big cayman snapped open his jaws and roared as the bullet ripped a furrow along the top of the armored skull, but didn't go through. The bullet broke and spattered against the stone parapet on the other side of the pool. Naked and still screaming the girls were running toward the house.

Christ! Lassiter cursed and tried for another careful shot. Roaring like something from hell, the maddened alligator was climbing out of the pool, while its tail whipped the blue water to froth. Lassiter fired again but the bullet didn't go through the eye; it chipped the thick ledge of bone above the eye, and ricocheted. The alligator dropped over the wall and began to charge.

It wasn't able to move as fast as a grizzly or a crazed cow buffalo. It was fast enough to make cold sweat pop out on Lassiter's face. The gator's stumpy clawed feet came rasping through leaves and hard-packed dirt. It was no more than twenty feet away when it opened its jaws and roared. Lassiter steadied the rifle and sent two bullets crashing down its throat. The gator was dead, but carried forward by its weight it didn't stop moving until it was close enough for Lassiter to smell the rotting breath from its jaws.

Looking at the dead cayman, he sleeved the sweat from his face and began to thumb a fresh load of shells into the Winchester. He thought he could use a drink along about now.

Spencer and the others came through the orange grove with leveled rifles, and the Irishman's eyes bugged out when he saw the dead alligator. "By Criekey!" he said. "To think they make suitcases out of them things."

"We thought you ran into an ambush," Spencer said, poking the gator with the muzzle of his rifle. Lassiter wondered how many books on alligators Spencer had read. "They're not supposed to be man-eaters," Spencer said. "But once they get a taste for it they never want anything else."

Lassiter grinned at him. "You don't say?"

A tall thin sallow old man with short white hair and a clipped mustache came around the hedge of jasmine with an old percussion revolver in his hand. He wasn't used to running, and two bright spots of red burned in his fever-yellowed face; between his white hair and white mustache the coal-black eyebrows looked strange. He was dressed like a rich Mexican, but instead of a sombrero he wore a wide-brimmed Guayaquil hat.

Spencer had his foot on the alligator's head, and the old man seemed to think he had killed the monster. Grabbing Spencer's hand in both of his own, he thanked him again and again in Spanish. There was nothing he wouldn't do for him, nothing he couldn't ask for. Embarrassed, Spencer pointed to Lassiter.

Lassiter didn't want the old gent pawing at him, so he backed away. Speaking his saloon Spanish, he said it was nothing. He was honored to have had the opportunity of saving the two lovely ladies from the cayman. Grinning inside, he had to fight to keep his face straight.

Suddenly the old man looked surprised. *"Y son esos Americanos?"* (And you are Americans?)

"More or less," Lessiter answered. "Some of us are Swedes and Irishmen." He wondered why it was taking the girls so long to get dressed and over their fright. Lord, he sure could use a drink, and to press it a little he unstoppered his canteen and took a sip of water. One day away from the ship, the water already had a metallic taste.

"A thousand pardons," the old man protested, sticking the old cap and ball pistol into his red sash. "This is no moment for water. Wine—whatever you wish to have. Come in, this way, gentlemen—my house is yours."

He bustled stiffly ahead of them, waving them

around to the opening in the bank of yellow jasmine. "My house—everything I have—is yours."

Even if the old gent meant it, Lassiter didn't think it was much of a reward for saving two beautiful senoritas. He was familiar with huts and haciendas in Northern Mexico, but this one was new to him. It looked more like a big birdcage than a house. Mostly it was a frame with open spaces; wall-sized bamboo blinds could be rolled down to keep out the sun and let in the breeze. It was one big room, wide and long, with a few chairs and tables bleached by salt air and sun. The floor was scrubbed down to the grain and covered with clean white sand. It rasped under their boots as they followed the old man inside.

He gave his name as Francisco Escobar Almirante, and as a matter of custom he was addressed as Don Francisco. "Ah, you are puzzled," he said to Lassiter. He laughed and pointed to the floor. "My house is down there. In the hot weather, and it is nearly always hot, it is more comfortable under the ground. And much safer when the northers come. This way, gentlemen."

At the end of the room a heavy wooden trapdoor was open and held in place with an iron hook. They followed Don Francisco downstairs and into a long, large room with whitewashed walls decorated with bright Mexican colors. The floor was of brick worn smooth by long use. There were time-darkened paintings in faded gilt frames that might have come all the way from Spain, and the light from three crystal chandeliers was reflected by floor to ceiling mirrors at both ends of the room. The mirrors made the room seem as long as a railroad station. Doors opened off the main room, and Lassiter wondered where the girls were.

Don Francisco was quietly proud of his elegant dugout. *"Pasen adentro,"* he waved them toward a polished mahogany table. Time had turned it from dark brown to glittering black. Spencer walked over to look at the portraits, but the rest of them sat down. Rasmussen, the Dane, and Kinsella, the dancing Irishman, looked confused. Lassiter thought Norstad was looking around for something he could steal. Sheep Callaway wasn't doing anything.

Don Francisco picked up a silver bell from the end of the table and set up a musical clatter. A thin Mexican woman with a weary face came bustling in, but the old man dismissed her. "My daughters shall serve you," he told Lassiter. "It was—perhaps still is —a custom in my native country—Spain. We can do no less for you."

Don Francisco bowed and Lassiter nodded. He'd be damned if he'd bow, no matter what the occasion. A thought came to him. Out there somewhere, maybe not so far away, Sandoval and his rebels were burning down the country, but you'd never know it from looking at the old man.

Don Francisco clapped his bony hands, and his voice got sharp. *"Niñas, vengan acá."* (Children, come here.)

Lassiter knew that Lupe was the dark one's name. She came in with her sister, and they bowed when the old man made the introductions. They were Lupe and Linda. Lassiter knew that Linda meant "pretty" in Spanish, that Lupe was short for Guadalupe. Hell, they were both pretty, but if he had to make a choice he'd like to put his brand on the dark one. As the fellas on the waterfront said, he liked the cut of her jib. Lupe had a real nice jib—she knew how to make it wobble, in a ladylike way, naturally—and the rest of her was just as good.

Custom called for them to kiss his hand, and they did. Lupe was second and she held his hand with her own while she kissed it. *"Nuestro salvador,"* (Our savior) she murmured with hooded eyes, but there was nothing subdued in her manner. There was something hostile in her eyes, a sort of mannish stride in her walk, and every time she looked at her sister a thin smile twitched across her lips. Lassiter guessed Linda and Lupe to be half-sisters: same father, different mothers. And maybe the differences between the two girls ran deeper than that.

Don Francisco hurried forward clapping his hands, telling his *niñas* to get moving with dinner. "Our friends are famished—hurry, hurry!"

Chapter Eight

"Senores, vamos a comer," Don Francisco called
out in a hearty voice. Translated, that meant come
on, gents—dig in.

Lassiter hadn't seen so much food since the time
he stuck-up the business men's banquet in Gold
Hill, Nevada. Those mine owners had done all right
by their bellies that night, but Don Francisco was
giving them some fair competition.

At that point they were expected to compliment
the old man on his grub. Lassiter was the only one
who spoke Spanish, so he did it. He grinned at
Spencer and said, "How come a college man like you
is so ignorant?"

It was nothing, Don Francisco protested, raising
his funny looking eyebrows as if to say he couldn't
believe that anyone could think the food on his huge
table wasn't as everyday as coffee and doughnuts in
a three-stool restaurant. He went on about it, saying
that he knew they might eat his humble fare to be
polite—but they wouldn't like it. Alas, he said in

Spanish, it was all he had, the best he could d
They must make allowances; he was ashamed.

"Ask him about . . ." Spencer was stopped by
hard look from Lassiter.

Lassiter said later.

First, the girls brought in turtle soup, and whe
that was gone, they loaded the table with fish an
the hot stuff the Mexicans called *chile relleno*.
they didn't like the wine on the table, then the
could have champagne, the old man said.

"Try the iguana steak," he said to Lassiter. Do
Francisco's thin lips twitched slightly, and maybe h
liked Americans, as he said he did, and maybe h
didn't.

Lassiter wasn't sure he liked the old man. "I don'
mind lizard when it tastes like chicken."

"Ah, you have been to Mexico before?"

"Not this far south. Sonora, Chihuahua, one tri
down to Baja California."

"And how do you like it? And why aren't yo
drinking?"

"Got any tequila?" Lassiter asked. "I like Mexic
fine."

Don Francisco said there must be a bottle o
tequila somewhere in the house.

Lupe found a bottle, dusted it off, and filled
glass for Lassiter. Spencer was trying to piece to
gether a sentence for the old man; the others wer
talking, so she was able to say it again without bein
heard. Leaning so close to Lassiter that her breas
touched his arm, Lupe said, *"Nuestro salvador."*

"Any time," Lassiter said.

He shook his head when the old man tried to pres
more food on him. It was good tequila—good *an*

ld, which was something new to him—and he
ipped at it while Norstad and the Irishman made
igs of themselves with dessert. Linda brought in
ranges, grapes, bananas, pitahaya, cherimolla cus-
ard.

"Cigars," Don Francisco announced. "And now I
hall ask the ladies to join us. In England I believe it
s the custom for ladies to retire once the cigars are
assed around. Not here."

Lassiter said he liked the Mexican customs better
han the English. "Sandoval been giving you any
rouble?" he asked as if the thought had just come
o him.

The old man didn't answer immediately, and
naybe he hadn't heard the question. Like hell he
adn't. Lassiter waited while Don Francisco waved
igars around, saying they could smoke Havanas, or
˙ they found Havanas too mild, they could try na-
ive cigars—Campeacheanos. "But I can't recom-
end them."

"I have had no trouble with Sandoval," the old
nan told Lassiter through a blue cloud of smoke.
In a way I am like the *negritos* you must have seen
n your way here. I am no friend of Sandoval nor of
he American companies he is fighting. I don't even
now what Sandoval looks like, but we have an
greement. Besides"—Don Francisco's voice got
ard—"I have the men to deal with him if he breaks
he agreement."

Lassiter said he hadn't seen any men.

"Most are at my rancho a few miles west of here.
Vhen the herd is branded and ready to move we will
rive it to Puerto Progreso in Yucatan." Don Fran-
isco delicately removed a shred of tobacco from his

old-man's yellow teeth. He sighed. "Santa Clara is only miles away, but with this recent trouble the American cattle boats have stopped coming."

"Then Sandoval *is* making trouble for you?"

Don Francisco smiled thinly. "I'm sure he doesn't mean to. I am well known and widely respected in the Territory of Quintana Roo. The American companies have caused their own share of trouble—their saw mills, their noisy machines. We had bandits before they came—a few bandits—and now we have something like a war."

Spencer asked Lassiter what the old man was going on about.

"He thinks American business men push too hard and their machines make too much noise." Lassiter took a chance that Don Francisco spoke no English. But he noticed that Lupe had a hard look in her eyes. They were inclined to be hard, so maybe he was wrong.

"He thinks he's the only aristocrat in Quintana Roo." Lassiter said. "Maybe he sees himself as the King of Quintana Roo. I think he'd like the business pirates and Sandoval to jump in the sea."

Sandoval's name made the old man look up.

Lassiter told the truth. "We came down here to kill Sandoval. Maybe you don't like that?"

Don Francisco said it was none of his business. All he wanted was to live in peace. He had built up a great ranch and wanted nothing more than to enjoy the fruit of his labors. His creaky voice got playful when he turned and spoke to his daughters. "To find suitable husbands for my girls—then I can die in peace."

"You have no son?"

"Alas, no."

Lassiter expressed his regrets, then asked Don Francisco if he would sell them some horses. He said they had come to kill Sandoval, but it wasn't working out that way. He said they needed more than thirty horses. He didn't want to take advantage of Don Francisco's kindness, but they needed horses.

"I'm afraid I can't help you," the old man said firmly. Then he smiled. "To sell—to give—you horses would break my agreement with Sandoval. However"—the old man was a bit of an actor—"if you were to steal some of my horses . . . That would be another matter." He made a chuckling noise in the back of his leathery throat. "If you were to take them by force, well then what could Sandoval say?"

"Not a thing, Don Francisco."

"I forbid you to take my horses, Señor Lassiter. I warn you: do not even go near my ranchero five miles west of here, along the Rio Bacalar."

Lassiter said they wouldn't think of doing such a thing.

"Of course you'll spend the night here? It's getting late and it looks like a storm. I think you'd better." A clap of the old man's hands brought the Mexican woman at a dead run. "When these gentlemen are ready, you will show them to their rooms."

"Not all of them," Lassiter said, jerking his thumb at Norstad, Rasmussen, Kinsella.

They were to stand the first watch, he said. Don Francisco protested, saying there was absolutely no need, but Lassiter pressed it. "Orders from Commodore Ambrose Ruffin, the dry goods sailor."

The fat man's name wasn't familiar to Don Francisco and he didn't get the joke. But he did understand the need for following orders. And if there was anything they needed during the night—anything at all . . .

Loosened up with tequila, Lassiter wondered how the old geezer would take it if he asked for the use of just one of his beautiful daughters. Linda, the shy one, had taken a mild shine to Spencer. Lassiter didn't mind that. Now Lupe—there was a girl.

The servant appeared again and the old man said, "*Señores, pasen ustedes buenas noches,*" which meant, Gentlemen, may you pass a pleasant night.

After days of smells and clatter on the *Judah P. Benjamin* Lassiter was ready to do just that. It wasn't a gentlemanly thing to do, but he snagged the bottle of tequila from the dining room table before he stood up. Linda giggled and Lupe looked interested. Lassiter explained it: "An old touch of malaria. Tequila is the only thing that helps."

Don Francisco, stiff but gracious, understood perfectly.

The bed in Lassiter's room was high and wide with a canopy on top. Getting into that bed would be like climbing on top of a half-filled captive balloon. The room was bare and clean, the kind he liked but so seldom slept in. Nothing was in it but the canopied bed, a few bright rugs on the polished brick floor, a Mexican Christ on the wall, a small table and one high-backed chair. A short, thick candle burned in a hand-made tin candlestick on a table beside the bed. There were matches to go with the candle. Lassiter tested one and it lit.

He took off his clothes and climbed onto the huge bed. Something rustled under the pillow, but it wasn't a scorpion, just a little cloth sack full of dried

110

flowers. With the uncorked bottle where he could reach it, he smoked one of Don Francisco's Havana cigars. The blue-gray smoke thinned out the flower scented air coming from the ventilation shaft. When his mind switched from the underground room he was in to the solitary cell in New Orleans, he got a closed-in feeling, but it passed after another drink.

He was thinking of Lupe—he still favored the dark over the light—when the door opened and she came in. A little drunk by now, Lassiter said in English: "Now who says God isn't good?"

In Spanish she told him to blow out the light.

Well, she might be there to slip a dirk between his ribs. She sure as hell wasn't there to talk because she could have talked without taking off her clothes. There was no mistaking the sound; hot country or not, these south Mexican girls wore too much clothing; she was stripping down to the buff. It took a while, long enough for Lassiter to have two more drinks.

When the last petticoat rustled to the floor, she moved forward in the darkness, saying: "My father would kill me if he . . ."

"Let's don't tell him," Lassiter said to her in Spanish, using both hands to pull her into bed. The best he could tell, she wasn't carrying anything deadlier than herself—come to think of it, she was deadly enough—and unless she meant to break his back, there was no good reason to think she was there to kill him.

"Not merely whip me, my father would . . ." Lupe said, laying hands on Lassiter. For a señorita raised by a strict Spanish father on an isolated hacienda, somehow this girl had managed to gain considerable experience.

Before Lassiter gave all his attention to the business at hand, he moved the .44 over to his side of the bed. Lupe spoke of the cayman, and Lassiter guessed the shudder she gave was genuine. Her voice was a murmur in the total darkness of the underground room. Cool night air from the shaft blew away the last of the cigar smoke, and once again the room smelled of flowers. Her roving hands built up tension in both of them, and she spoke more rapidly. He was a good and brave man, she said, a gallant man far from home, from family. Did he have a family and was he lonely?

"No family living that I know of."

"But you are lonely?"

"You bet," Lassiter said. Lordy, he thought, this one could make a fortune in New Orleans, if she ever decided to do it professionally.

She kissed him, nibbled at his lip, and there was no more talk for about fifteen minutes. It was cool in the dark room, but they were sweating when they finished and lay back on the stack of pillows. Lupe's long, black, perfumed hair had come loose; she laughed quietly while they searched for her silver combs.

"No light, I don't need a light," she told him. She worked on her hair, fixing it, coiling it. She was still in bed, but Lassiter knew the signs of departure.

"What's the hurry?" he asked. The roll in the hay had been such a humdinger that he didn't see why they couldn't rest up for a bit, then lock horns again.

"For me there is no hurry"—Lupe trembled—"but I must think of Papa. I will drink with you—a little drink—and then I must go."

She had her legs over the edge of the bed. "I will get the bottle—you rest."

Lassiter listened to the bottle being uncorked, the sound of drinking. He grinned at her coughing. "Awful stuff," she said. "How it burns." She gave the bottle to Lassiter and was ready to leave. She leaned forward to kiss him. "I hope I have pleased you."

Lassiter said if she wrote it, he'd sign it. The meaning of what he said sort of got lost when he translated it into Spanish, but Lupe got the idea. She said goodnight again and went out, and if Lassiter had been a fanciful fella he might have wondered if she had been there at all. But he wasn't and the smell of her was still around to prove that she had been there.

Smoking a last cigar before he settled in for the night, he listened to the rumble of faraway thunder, and before he was ready to quich his smoke, the storm had moved closer. Now when the thunder rolled it seemed to shake the underground hacienda, though the noise itself was muffled.

Lassiter grinned: it was a good night to be in a big soft bed after a tussle with a good-looking woman. Upstairs it would be raining like a son of a bitch, the heavy tropical rain driven by howling wind, but you'd never know it where he was. Yeah, he decided, he was a selfish bastard, not giving a damn about the boys standing guard. . . .

Chapter Nine

Lassiter woke up and reached for his gun and didn't find it. He always reached for his gun when something woke him in the night. For a moment he listened to the tail-end of the storm dragging itself away. Thunder still rolled like artillery in a distant battle, but he knew that wasn't what had jolted him from his sleep. After all the years of sleeping on the run, he knew that wasn't it.

After the first reach for the gun he didn't move again. He knew there was someone else in the blackened room, and though he lay motionless, holding his breath, he couldn't hear a sound. Though the storm was still rattling in the distance, it would have been possible to hear anything in the room—there was nothing.

No, that wasn't right: there was something: not a sound, more like the movement of something coming toward the bed. It was somebody putting one foot in front of the other on the floor, and there wasn't a sound. Lassiter knew that's what was happening, just as a moment later he knew the man who was there to kill him was standing beside the bed. Only half thinking about it, he knew that was peculiar because in all the years men had stalked him in the darkness, and he had done the same when it was called for, he couldn't remember a time when there hadn't been some noise—the whisper of breath, the rustling of cloth.

He made a snorting noise as though he had gone back to sleep. Idly he noticed that the room no longer smelled so strongly of flowers, that the air was cooler, more natural. Forcing himself to relax, he waited.

The knife came down without a sound, but he knew the blade was aimed for his chest; that it was meant to kill him. His hand reached up swiftly to stop the downcoming blow—toward where he hoped it was coming—and there was a muted grunt instead of a cry when his hand closed hard on a greasy wrist. His hand struck the wrist before it grabbed it, and the force of the downward thrust drove the knife blade against the inside of the arm and there was no pain as the steel sliced thinly through hard flesh and brought the trickle of blood.

No sound came after the first though the held back breath of the attacker gusted in Lassiter's face. He reached up to grab the other hand that should, by rights, be coming down to claw at his face, maybe to try to shift the knife from one hand to the other. But his upreaching left hand touched nothing, and he shifted it to close on the hand that held the descending knife. The years had thickened Lassiter's wrists and had given strength to his hands, but the man that held the knife that was trying to kill him was strong as a bull. Added to that, he was on his back and the killer had a downward thrust. He fought the coming-down push of the knife, and when he thought about it later he didn't know why he did it silently—why he didn't shout and yell for help.

His two hands were gripped hard on the greased wrist, and though he put ferocious effort into an attempt to turn the knife back, there wasn't even a quiver from the hand that was trying to put the blade through his heart. For a moment they held steady, the two of them, one trying to kill, the other determined not to die. It was a stand-off for longer than a moment, then Lassiter heard a wet, wheezing sound as the knifer's strength gave way and he sucked air into his lungs. The arm that held the knife trembled and so did the whole body behind it.

Thinking back later, Lassiter himself didn't know why he didn't yell and bring people running. Maybe the thought came and he got rid of it, or maybe it didn't come at all. Slowly the pressure of the down-thrusting arm began to weaken. It took time and all Lassiter's strength to get the silent struggle to that point. And just as slowly as the killer's downward thrust began to weaken, Lassiter turned the blade away from his chest. It came away from his chest, the point, and then the whole blade was level with his chest.

When the point of the knife was turning upward toward the killer, Lassiter said something that he couldn't remember later when he tried to think of it. It was in Spanish, and maybe it was a question or a word to spit in a killer's face. It didn't matter: there was no answer. All that came was the sound of breath sucked in fast, the stink of sweat mixed with grease. Lassiter's mouth was dry, but he spat as much as he could in the knifer's face—and that didn't bring any reaction.

Lassiter cursed and felt rage jumping in his head. The son of a bitch was trying to pull his hand free, but Lassiter's straining hands held the wrist like a vice. Seconds, maybe full minutes, ticked by in his brain as slowly he turned the knife. The blade came up until it was flat and level between them, then it began to move upward toward the attacker's chest. Then suddenly there was strange, grunting cry and the knifer pushed himself onto the knife. That was all right with Lassiter and he was ready to help this fella make an end of himself. If the point got stuck on a bone, he'd just have to yank it clear and make a better job of it. But the blade went in straight and easy, and Lassiter knew it had found the heart because the greasy wrist his fingers were clamped on trembled with one last surge of life. Lassiter had killed other men with cold steel and you got to know when your man was shamming, when he was dead.

But a man stayed alive by being careful, and while he held the dead wrist tight with iron fingers, Lassiter reached up into the darkness with the other hand and pulled the knife out of the attacker's chest. It had gone through all the way to the haft and he had to turn it a ways before he could pull it clear. Only then did he turn loose the greasy wrist. It pulled away from him, and he heard the body hitting the bedside table. The dead man and the heavy table went over with a crash that echoed through the underground house.

Lassiter got down on the floor and groped for the candlestick and the spilled matches. He found the candle still stuck in its holder and got it lit. Up above he heard dull, choked-off sounds that might have been shooting. With the .44 in his hand, he brought the guttering candle down low, to look at the man he had killed. He was setting the table back on its legs when he heard voices and footsteps hurrying down the tiled hallway outside.

Don Francisco, a gentleman even in a crisis, knocked on the door and asked permission to come in. Spencer, with Callaway behind him, pushed his way into the room. Both men had guns in their hands, and when Don Francisco followed them inside, he had a gun too: the same old cap and ball pistol.

"What in hell is that?" Spencer said, looking at the dead man.

Callaway just looked, didn't say anything.

"What was that shooting?" Lassiter asked.

Callaway said: "Somebody shot at the men on sentry. The Swede yelled down nobody was hit."

Don Francisco got close enough to move the dead man's leg with the toe of his boot. Some of the grease from the cooling body stuck to the leather and the old Spaniard looked disgusted. "I am disgraced," he said to Lassiter; a deep, frowning crease brought his thick black eyebrows close together. "That someone—this thing—should attack a guest under my roof . . ."

"You know him?" Lassiter asked in Spanish.

"Know him?" The idea, the question, infuriated Don Francisco.

Lassiter asked it another way. "I mean, have you ever seen him before?"

Don Francisco was positive: the answer was No.

"Nor do I know how he got into my house."

Callaway spoke up: "Not through the trapdoor. I'm not much for sleeping, so I set my chair and my rifle right at the bottom of the stairs that lead down. He didn't come in that way."

"The grease . . ." Spencer started to say, looking at Lassiter.

"That's right," Lassiter said. "Through the air shaft is how he came in."

Don Francisco protested in formal Spanish made even stiffer by outrage. "Impossible, my friend. Even the main shaft is too narrow."

Lassiter tore a strip from one of the pillowcases and wound it around the knife cut on his arm. "Look again," he told the old man. "Whoever he is or was, he's just a kid. Strong but small and skinny. They stripped him, greased him, sent him on through."

Callaway bent down to take a closer look at the corpse. The mournful man-catcher used his thumb to push back one of the dead man's eyelids. The eye had the blank stare of death, but Callaway asked Lassiter to pass him the candle.

Callaway brought the candle down until it was throwing a garish yellow light into the dead man's face. He thumbed back the other eyelid before he straightened up.

"This fella's blind," he said. "Many's the poor prisoner went blind working the summerfields at Huntsville. Brother, I ought to know."

To Lassiter, thinking about it, it figured. A fella had to do everything the first time. And this was his first time to kill a greased-down, one-armed Mexican blindman.

That seemed to convince Don Francisco and,

attling in Spanish so fast that Lassiter could under-
tand only an occasional word, the old man cocked
is pistol and swore that he would stand guard over
Señor Lassiter for the rest of the night.

Lassiter said that was most honorable of his
onored host. For a fella who had learned most of
is Spanish in Tex-Mex saloons and whorehouses, it
ook some doing to translate all that honorable
ullcrap, but he managed.

Going out of the room revolver at the ready, Don
'rancisco protested that it was nothing. For having
een so careless as to allow a murderer to sneak into
is house, would gladly die in defense of his honored
uests.

With a tight grin, Lassiter listened to the last of
Don Francisco's protestations. Then he winked at
Spencer, who still looked sick to his stomach. "You
hink the old gent is mixed up in this, Spencer?"

"That's ridiculous," Spencer said. "The man's a
entleman."

"Yeah," Lassiter agreed, thinking of other
entlemen he'd known.

Lassiter and Callaway went topside and found
Don Francisco standing guard, the heavy pistol rest-
ng in the crook of his arm. The storm had moved on
outh and the wind had moved the oily-black clouds
o let the moon shine through. The trees close to the
ouse still dripped; the soaked earth gave off a sweet-
sh smell.

"Yo," Norstad called out in reply to Lassiter's
ail. Rasmussen and Kinsella yelled too. They were
ll right, but didn't sound too happy about it. Las-
iter figured they would be happier breaking heads
n some Nevada mine strike.

123

"You think maybe they'll try another attack?" Callaway wanted to know.

"What attack. That first bit of shooting was just noise to ease the way for the blindman."

Callaway went to take up his guard position at one end of the open-framed house; after a few minutes Spencer came topside and hunkered down with his rifle at the other end. Lassiter took the center of the house, on the side facing away from the hedge of jasmine. He was chewing on a cold, tightly rolled cigarette when Don Francisco left his place at the trapdoor and came over to say something.

Lassiter looked sideways at the old man, who seemed to be having trouble putting his words together. Out in the darkness the parched countryside had soaked up the cloudburst like a sponge, and except for the fading drip of water from the sides of the house, the storm might never have happened.

"That rain ought to do some good," Lassiter began. Discussing the weather wasn't one of his strong points, but he couldn't think of much else to say. He was glad to see that Don Francisco had uncocked his pistol and stuffed it back into his sash. The old gent had calmed down a bit and might have something interesting to say.

What Don Francisco said was: "Men fear these storms, but what would this hot country do without them?" The old man's tone was solemn; as if the same observation hadn't been made a million times since the beginning of the world.

Holding back a grin, Lassiter said, "Right you are."

A sharp intake of breath told Lassiter that Don Francisco was ready to say his piece.

124

"I am forever in your debt, Señor Lassiter," the old man began. "All I have worked and lived for would be gone without you. My daughters . . ."

Lassiter glanced at the old man standing awkwardly to one side. What had happened earlier in the night had a bad smell and maybe the old man had some part in it. He was ready to hear more testimony before he brought in a verdict of guilty.

"You risked your life to save not one but both my children . . ."

"You said thanks already," Lassiter reminded the old Spaniard. "That's not your way. You're thanking me again because you think I think you set me up to be killed."

"Is that what you think?"

"Well it wouldn't be the first time it's happened."

Lassiter moved the Winchester a few inches when the old man's hand reached for the butt of his revolver. It came out of the sash in a slow, awkward movement. Don Francisco might well be a gentleman, as he claimed, but sure as hell he was no fast draw.

"Hey, hold on there, Pappy," Lassiter said quickly when, instead of pointing the pistol at him, the old man cocked it and placed the muzzle about where he thought his heart might be. Remembering that Don Francisco didn't speak English, he said something like it in Spanish, leaving off the Pappy. These Mexicans and Spaniards made a fuss about honor, but doing the Dutch act was carrying it too far.

"What else can I do?" the old man asked in a dull voice. "You have not shamed me, I have shamed myself. You were a guest in my house and . . ."

"Put it away. Nobody is blaming you. I figure a Spanish gentleman like you wouldn't be up to such sneaky tricks as a yellow dog like Sandoval would pull. A man like you would have nothing to do with scum like that."

Suddenly the old man uncocked his pistol and put it away. A change of tone showed in his voice when he said: "Sandoval is one man, I am another. Once again you must believe I had nothing to do with the attack on your life."

Why not? Lassiter said, "Your word's good enough."

That seemed to settle the old man's nerves. "To-morrow you will go to my ranchero. Before you leave I will send Lupe ahead to order the men away from there. Take the animals you need: no one will try to stop you."

Nothing happened for the rest of the night, and when the sun came up, a burning red ball in the eastern sky, Don Francisco was still on guard, the percussion pistol in his belt.

Lassiter had never seen such a tired old Spaniard.

Chapter Ten

The killing of the blind man had soured the festive air of Don Francisco's hacienda. Lassiter, Spencer and the others pulled up their chairs to the big table. Breakfast was served by the fat servant woman they had seen the night before.

Silver bristles glistened on Don Francisco's bony chin as he took his place at the head of the table. Linda, the blond daughter, was late getting to the table and the old man frowned slightly without saying anything.

"You must forgive the appearance of things," Don Francisco said in Spanish to Lassiter while including the rest of them, especially Spencer, with a humorless smile. "Our life here has always been tranquil. We are not accustomed to . . ."

Lassiter went after the fried meat and honeycakes. He looked over at Linda, who had no appetite at all for a growing girl, and if she had any smiles left, they were shy and mostly directed at Spencer.

Lupe came into the room all dressed to go riding.

The hardness that Lassiter had noticed the night before had been hardened some more by the mannish looking riding clothes she was wearing. Down in South America the more active females wore what they called gaucho skirts—pants that could be taken for skirts—but the way Lupe walked the things she wore just had to be called pants. And there was no nonsense about the deerskin waist-jacket, the up-to-the-elbow leather gloves, the flat-crowned brushed-leather hat with the wide brim. Lassiter had seen less fancy outfits in an Annie Oakley Show, but if Lupe was carrying a pistol it didn't show.

All she did was nod as she passed the table, then through the long room, on her way to the trapdoor. A sharp word from the old man turned her around. It looked like Don Francisco wanted her to thank his guests one more time. Lupe didn't like it and Lassiter could see her point. No need for her to go on thanking these gringo heroes till her tongue got dry.

But she did because that's what the old man wanted. Norstad, Kinsella and Rasmussen, not understanding a word of Spanish, just mumbled or grunted Spencer, the fool, made a sitting-down bow. Then Lupe thanked Lassiter, her savior, but her eyes stayed hard.

They dragged out breakfast because the idea was to give Don Francisco's men enough time to ride away from the *ranchero*. They finished eating and the fat woman fetched out brandy and cigars, tequila for Lassiter. That used up about thirty minutes more. Lassiter downed his third drink and said it was time to go.

Don Francisco and Linda went topside with them and waved as they moved away from the hacienda.

Lassiter had nothing to say to Linda; what could he say even if the old man hadn't been there? Spencer kept looking at the blond girl and clearing his throat. Finally, after Lassiter prodded him in the ribs, he walked away from the house.

With good food and strong brandy in his belly, Kinsella, the Irishman, was ready to turn sentimental. "Lord Almighty, Mr. Lassiter," he said in his wheedling voice. "I hate like hell to leave that there hacienda."

Lassiter grinned at the Irishman. "Don't tell me, paddy. Tell *Mister* Spencer—he's hurting more than you are. Blonds on the brain."

Without breaking his stride Spencer said, "You go to hell, you son of a bitch."

The sun was well up in the sky, but not high enough yet to start the sweat popping. A whisper of breeze stirred the yellow-green grass of the vast rangeland beyond the house. Lassiter felt pretty good for a man who was still alive on a morning he should have been dead with a cut-through heart.

"Go with God, my son," he told Spencer, putting a freshly rolled cigarette between his teeth and pausing to fire up a match on a thickened thumbnail.

They moved ahead in single file through the sea of grass. Norstad took the point; followed by Kinsella, Rasmussen and Spencer.

Callaway was behind Lassiter. "Yeah?" he said when Callaway moved up beside him. Off to the west the low, jagged mountains—the last gasp of the Rockies, that ran from the cold snows of Canada to this burned-over sink, showed themselves a grayish-blue in the shimmering distance. While the sun was early up, it was possible to make a close guess at how far away the mountains were. Now, with the sun climbing higher, near to the noon mark, a man couldn't trust his guess.

"Never knew you were the trusting kind," Callaway started.

"That a fact?"

"Maybe we should have taken the old greaser, the two girls. Wouldn't be that much trouble, Lassiter."

"Maybe more than you know. You want to take hostages, brother, you go back and take them. Hostages for what, brother? Maybe you can tell me?"

"No, brother, you're the smart fella in this outfit."

"I'll tell you one thing, convict. Taking that old man captive—or one of the daughters—isn't the way out of this. That's my feeling. Now you get back in line."

Moving at a good clip, they followed the north bank of the sluggish river the old man had called Rio Bacalar, and in the places where it spread out to form swampland, alligators stirred and crunched in the reeds. Maybe fifty miles wide from north to south, the prairie ran flat and straight all the way to the distant mountains. That's what it looked like from where they were, but Lassiter knew that every prairie had hollows and gullies where a hundred men could hide. Touching a match to a cigarette without breaking his stride, he thought back on his conversation with the old man. Maybe—just maybe—the old gent was a man of honor, as he claimed so strongly. Put on the scales, Don Francisco's word of honor did seem to have some weight. So they still might ride away from this present trouble without any extra holes in their hides.

About three miles from Don Francisco's place—

and now they could see the *ranchero* maybe two miles ahead—Lassiter called a halt. After taking a swig from his canteen, Norstad pointed out what Lassiter had already seen: a bunch of mounted men moving away west from the *ranchero*. That would be Don Francisco's vaqueros doing what Lupe had been sent to tell them.

After that it took less than an hour to get within shouting distance of the *ranchero*. Spread out wide, they came in slow; down on their bellies in the waving grass they waited for Lassiter's word to move in.

It looked about the way he thought it would look: a regular corral with maybe heavier posts and railings than you'd find up north. In one corner of the corral there was a shack built of peeled poles and thatched with palm leaves. That would be the shack where they store lassos, saddles, other gear. The shack was too small to hold more than a few men at one time, and that wasn't what bothered Lassiter.

Squinting along the barrel of his Winchester, Callaway put words to what Lassiter was thinking about the horses crowded together in one corner of the corral.

"Fine looking animals, brother," Callaway remarked easily. "Only they don't look even half broke."

"Maybe not that much," Lassiter said, thinking that the deal with the old man called for animals they could saddle and steal in a hurry—for animals they could ride.

While he was thinking about it, the bunched up horses—mustangs was the right word—broke loose from the corner of the corral and started in with some mean-and-fancy bucking and running. And they hadn't even got close yet.

"Well, boys," Lassiter said, "we're here and they're there. Everybody move in and steal himself a pony. Then learn to stay on his back."

"Over that way," Callaway said to Lassiter, pointing with the barrel of his rifle. "Riders coming in fast."

"Yeah, I see them. Move inside and take up positions."

Still too far out for accurate shooting, the Mexicans weren't all out of the gullies that hid them when the riders in front started throwing lead. The bullets sang wide and high as they headed for the corral at a dead run. They made the rail and everybody got over it except the bulky Irishman who tried to go under and got struck. Lassiter kicked him through and Kinsella said thanks. Kinsella, Norstad and Rasmussen took one side; Lassiter, Callaway and Spencer took the other.

The Mexicans were closer, with the bullets finding the range. Callaway yelled out, "Christ, they got lances!"

Lassiter didn't know what Callaway had against lances. "If they get close enough to use those pig-stickers, then we're done for."

A bugle brayed and Sandoval's bandit cavalry came at them fast and loud, yelling, *"Mueran los Yankees"* (Death to the Yankees.) Lassiter grinned sourly and sighted along the barrel of his rifle. With the sun so high and bright the metal threw back a glare, and he wet his thumb, dipped it in dust and dulled the brightness of the barrel.

"About fifteen seconds more," he called out. It looked like they were about to pay for the crimes of